THE CRIMES OF ALICE BOOK ONE

FROM USA TODAY BESTSELLING AUTHOR
ERIN BEDFORD

Also by Erin Bedford

The Underground Series
Chasing Rabbits
Chasing Cats
Chasing Princes
Chasing Shadows
Chasing Hearts
The Crimes of Alice
Hatter's Heart

The Mary Wiles Chronicles
Marked by Hell
Bound by Hell
Deceived by Hell
Tempted by Hell

Starcrossed Dragons
Riding Lightning
Grinding Frost
Swallowing Fire
Pounding Earth

The Crimson Fold
Until Midnight
Until Dawn
Until Sunset

Curse of the Fairy Tales
Rapunzel Untamed
Rapunzel Unveiled
Rapunzel Unchained

<u>Her Angels</u>

Heaven's Embrace
Heaven's A Beach
Heaven's Most Wanted

<u>House of Durand</u>

Indebted to the Vampires
Wanted by the Vampires
Protected by the Vampires
Embrace of the Vampires
Tempted by the Butler
Loved by the Vampires
Huntress of the Vampires

<u>Academy of Witches</u>

Witching On A Star
As You Witch
Witch You Were Here
Just Witch It
Summer Witchin'

<u>Children of the Fallen</u>

Death In Her Eyes
Fire In Her Blood

The Beast of the Fae Court
Granting Her Wish
Vampire CEO

TABLE OF CONTENTS

HATTERS HEART

THE CRIMES OF ALICE BOOK ONE

FROM USA TODAY BESTSELLING AUTHOR
ERIN BEDFORD

COMPLAINTS AND COHORTS

MY MOTHER WOULD HAVE adored Mrs. Tara McAllister. She was everything she expected a woman to be in the nineteenth century. Besides the fact that the human sitting across from my desk wore a pantsuit instead of a gown.

Pantsuits were the equivalent to dresses for well-to-do women in the twenty-first century. She was articulated, gossipy, but in a hushed way, and overly concerned by anyone not abiding by the rules.

As my friend Kat would say, "Fuck the rules."

I hated to think I would have been an exact replica of Mrs. McAllister had I stayed in the nineteenth century. God forbid, if I had actually married Lewis.

Suppressing a shudder, I shifted in my chair, hoping she hadn't noticed my drifting attention.

"And while I have nothing against you fairy folk," Mrs. McAllister shifted in her seat and fluffed her dyed blonde hair, "but I don't understand how the president even allows those creatures to integrate with polite society."

I adjusted the collar of my own blush colored suit jacket and tried not to sigh.

Mrs. McAllister quickly added, "Not you, Alice, dear. I mean those..." her nose scrunched up with obvious disgust, "...trolls, those ugly little faeries, and while I do appreciate the cleanliness of the brownies, they leave a lot to be desired in the looks department, don't you agree?"

I nodded politely but didn't comment.

"They're not like you and the other representatives." She smiled softly, her eyes getting that far off look most got when talking about the higher fae. "While I do not care for that Katherine young lady, her mother and I were in the same social groups for a while, before her daughter became one of *them*."

I tried ignore the fact that she had once again forgotten I too was Fae. I ran into a lot of her kind before I became Fae myself. It was one of the reasons I wanted to be stay in the Underground rather than the human realm.

One of my best friends, Katherine or rather Kat, lived in the human realm most of her life too before she found out she was actually the reincarnation of the Seelie Princess. Then she ended up just as deep in the Fae world as I had found myself to be. It was even worse now that the Fae were out of the literal portal.

"Now that Erydesa," Mrs. McAllister continued, "she's a wonderful woman. If only all you Fae were like her. The way she handled Congress—"

"Mrs. McAllister," I interrupted her, ready to be done with this. "I will bring your complaint up with the Moderator, Katherine. I'm sure we can find a reasonable solution to your faerie problem." I pushed back from the table and stood, not giving her the chance to argue with me as I held my hand out. "Thank you for bringing this to our attention and please feel free to bring any other concerns in the future."

The woman scrambled to her feet and shook my hand, her hands cold and clammy. "Oh, yes. Of course. Thank you for seeing me. Like I said, I have nothing against your kind, I just like my garden a specific way and those faeries -"

"Of course," I forced an agreeable smile to my lips and nodded, leading her to the door of my office. "We all do. Have a great day, Mrs. McAllister."

I ushered her out of my office and shut the door behind her. I waited a moment before sagging against the wood and sighed.

When I took the job as representative between the Fae and humans, I hadn't expected there to be so many complaints about little things. The trolls were falling asleep in the streets. The brownies kept sneaking into houses and cleaning them. The fucking faeries kept getting into every person in a hundred-mile radius's gardens and rearranging the flowers.

Now the majority of the population didn't seem to be bothered by the Fae at all. Of course, half of them were in awe of us still and the other half were scared. We had made leaps and bounds in the last year since the Fae had come out of the portal and into the human world. There were bound to be some people who weren't happy with our existence let alone us infiltrating their world.

Then there were the Mrs. McAllisters. For every human who liked or hated us, there was one in the middle who pretended to be okay with us but then would find everything they could to complain about. This was just one of the many Mrs. McAllisters I'd had to deal with today. Thankfully, she was the last.

Rubbing my temples, I slogged over to my desk and finished up the paperwork to log Mrs. McAllister's complaint. A half an hour later, I had my purse and was locking up the office.

When I had first accepted the job, I had been working out of Kat's kitchen. With myself as the go between of the two species, I brought all the complaints that I couldn't handle myself to Kat, who was acting Moderator on this side of the portal. Her other half, Chess, worked the Underground side. How they handled being separated so often was a miracle to me. I couldn't imagine being separated from my Hatter.

I smiled slightly at the thought of my serious but sweet man. He had taken living in the human world in stride. Supporting me and my work while he worked on...well, I wasn't quite sure what my paramour worked on while I was away. Hatter was always home when I arrived, but he had to do something while I was gone, didn't he? I would hate to think he was just sitting there all day bored out of his mind.

Though, compared to the Underground, the human world had many vices to keep one's interest. One of them being reality television. Hatter and I enjoyed watching those talk shows where the mother doesn't know who the father of her child is. Even better the hoarder shows, where they have to practically dig the human out of their own garbage.

We tried to get into some of those fantasy movies, but nothing quite settled right with having lived the very worlds they were pretending to be in. A lot of the time Hatter and I would be complaining about how unrealistic their fairies were. Really, fairies had other things to do than to go around helping children to fly.

Ridiculous.

Still, I'd have to ask Hatter when I got home. Before I did that, I had to go check in with Kat.

Walking down the road, I wished for the hundredth time that the modern vehicle wasn't sixty-five percent iron. Not that many humans knew this but Fae were highly allergic to iron. We played off our aversion to cars as wanting the exercise.

However, some days I almost would subject myself to the pain just to not have to walk home. We Fae have been in this world for a good year and still we haven't found an alternative source of transportation.

To my aching feet's delight, the walk to Kat's home was only a half an hour walk at best. It was much better than it used to be. I groaned as I remembered the hour long walk it took to get to Kat's old house. Thank the reaper, Kat had moved closer to town when her grandmother came back from vacation. Unfortunately, we couldn't move the portal closer to her new home. We still had to traipse out into the woods to go home to visit.

"Alice?" Kat's voice called out as I stalked up the front porch, my heels making a loud thumping sound. "Is that you?"

I grunted.

"Grunt once for yes and twice for no," Kat continued with a smile in her voice.

"I already grunted. If I grunt again that counts as no." I pursed my lips, I waited on the porch for her. I didn't have long to wait.

Kat threw open the front door, juggling two glasses of white wine and a wide grin on her face. "You are always so literal, Al. Can't you take a joke?"

I lifted my eyes to the roof. "Not when I'm in dire need of alcohol." Graciously, Kat handed over my glass of wine and we sat down on the porch swing.

Drinking at least half the glass, I sighed and leaned my head back on the swing.

"Bad day?"

I grunted once.

"Another well-to-do I'm not speciest but blah blah blah?" Kat smirked and sipped from her own glass, her pale blue eyes staring off into the distance.

I snorted, flipping my blonde hair over my shoulder. "Is there any other kind?"

One could almost say we were related, both of us blonde haired and blue eyed. Except any ninny with half a brain could tell my eyes were a darker blue and Kat's hair was more white than blonde. It was still better than that garish red hair she used to have before her Fae heritage came out.

"What were they complaining about this time?" Kat pushed the swing with her foot, curling the other one up and under her. She didn't bother wearing a pant suit or anything close to respectable. Her ripped jeans which she had paid for that way and white V-neck shirt with the words 'If you can read this, back the fuck up' in small black letters.

It still bothered me that she used such crude language as if it were a natural thing. Then again, the twenty-first century was far different than nineteenth century Cheshire, England, my hometown, and century of birth.

I was just lucky that the humans found my old-fashioned ways quaint and my accent adorable. It made it easy to get away with not knowing half of what they were saying.

Shrugging out of my suit jacket, the summer heat making my skin stick to my shirt underneath, I grumbled out, "Well, Mr. Dobs is tired of having to go the long way around town because of trolls sleeping on main street."

Kat scoffed. "Not surprising. It's probably Bar. He likes to hang out on Main Street near the toy shop. I'll talk to him about it tomorrow. What else?"

I ticked the complaints off on my fingers until I got to the last and latest complaint.

The moment Kat heard Mrs. McAllister's name she groaned. "Oh, fuck that old biddy. She just likes to complain. It's likely the faeries aren't anywhere near her garden and she just wanted to come make my life hell."

"Past grievances, I presume?" I hide a smile behind my wine glass.

Kat downed her glass of wine in one go and shook her head at me. "Don't get me started. I'll send my mother to deal with her."

"Which one?" I arched a brow.

Laughing like a hyena, Kat almost rolled off the swing. "It would serve her right if I sent the Seelie Queen after her." She paused and sighed, wiping the side of her eyes. "No, sadly, my human mother can put Mrs. McAllister in her place just as easily. I'll just point in her direction and -"

"I thought I'd find you out here, my pet." A low rolling purr interrupted Kat. From the darkening of her eyes and smile on her lips, I supposed she didn't mind.

"Hello, Cheshire." I turned in my seat to greet the pink haired Fae. "How are you this evening?"

"Alice." He nodded his head in my direction but his emerald eyes only for Kat. "I'm better now that I'm home."

Cheshire S. Cat was what Kat liked to call Sex on a Stick. The expression while strange stuck with me. Cheshire did have a sensual way to him that was so familiar to me that I felt a bit odd to even be attracted to him. Who could blame me though?

He kept his long pink hair braided and thrown over his shoulder. His purple and black striped ears twitching on top of his head were just as distracting as the matching tail he kept wrapped around his waist. Those were the only attributes that even made his surname make sense. Supposedly, his father was able to morph into a full feline, but no one has seen him in years. Still, Cheshire reminded me more of the pirates I'd read about when I was a child, all tight pants, and billowing tops. How anyone took him seriously was beyond my comprehension.

"Chess," Kat slid from the swing and sauntered over to her lover. His hands wrapped around her hips, drawing her close as Kat slid her hands up and into the opening neck of his shirt. "I missed you," Kat murmured before there were definite kissing sounds.

I turned my head, my cheeks flushing. Finishing off my glass of wine, I hopped to my feet and pulled my purse over my shoulder. "I better be going. Hatter will be waiting for me, no doubt."

Pausing from their reunion, Kat twisted to look at me. "Why do you keep calling him that? You know his name, don't you?"

"Well, yes." I frowned.

"Moradoc is gone, there's no reason to keep using his nickname." Kat released Chess and walked over to me, her hands taking me by the arms. "He can't hurt anymore, you know that right?"

I nodded, my eyes down on the ground. "Yes, but he still hasn't been caught. He could come back and then —"

"He's trapped in the Shadow Realm. There's no way he could come back. Besides," she smiled and brushed my hair out of my face, "They'd have to get through the Reaper and us first, and he knows what happened last time." Green veins lit up along her skin as magic pooled into her hand.

Forcing myself to relax and smile, I tried to show her I was alright. "You're right. Of course. I'm just being paranoid. I'll let you two get reacquainted. See you tomorrow?"

Frowning slightly at me, Kat gave me a quick hug. "Of course. Call me if you need anything, you still remember how?"

I suppressed a sigh. "Yes. For the hundredth time. I know how to use a cell phone. I also have the mirror phone as well."

"Good." She smacked me on the arm, making me wince. "Use them."

Not commenting on her boorish actions, I waved slightly at Cheshire before making my way down the steps to start the long trek home.

OUR HOUSE SAT ABOUT two miles away from Kat's, a bit away from the street. One of the main aspects I loved about the place was the long walkway up to the Victorian style house. It reminded me of my childhood home. Or what I remembered of it.

We hadn't done much to the house since we acquired it. Hatter — or rather Mercury — had said I could change anything I liked and with magic at our disposal changing the colors of walls or flooring was quite easy and affordable. Magic couldn't fix the more complicated changes such as knocking down walls and updating the plumbing. That was when my job as representative came in handy.

I had never in my wildest dreams thought I would have a job, let alone my own bank account. I certainly wouldn't have had one had I not fallen into that rabbit hole. Not that I regret it. I missed my family sometimes of course, but I didn't remember them much. I blamed the Seelie Queen for that bit. Being imprisoned for hundreds of years will do things to a person's minds. Even a Fae.

Glancing down at my hand, I pushed magic into my nails, changing the color from a nude to a pretty pale blue. A part of me still expected for my magic to disappear one of these days. I hadn't done much in my life to deserve it and the deal I made to get it had been with the Shadow Man or Moradoc. My part in the whole ordeal was one of the reasons I took the position as representative to make up for all the heartache and pain I caused.

Sighing with a sort of satisfaction that made my feet skip, I went up the walkway. Curiously, the lights were off in the two-story house. My enhanced hearing didn't pick up any sound from inside the house other than the electricity and the air conditioner running.

Had Hat — Mercury gone out?

Normally, he would tell me if he was going anywhere. As I opened the front door, I pulled my cell phone from my purse. Pressing on the screen, I waited for it to come to life.

No messages or missed calls.

Frowning further, I wandered through the house in search of him. "Mercury?" I peeked my head into his workshop but found his seat at the worktable empty, unfinished hats set aside, and spools of ribbons strewn across the room. If I hadn't known the man, I'd have said there was a struggle, but Mercury's creative process wasn't something I could comprehend.

Some nights he spent hours in his shop and sometimes didn't come out with anything new at all. There were other nights he would have made several different hats for some of his special request clients but seem completely torn by the prospect of parting with them.

I supposed it would be hard to separate from one's work of art for money. I'd told him before he didn't have to do it, but he insisted on contributing to the household.

"I promised to take care of you, little one." Mercury's smooth voice caressed my ears as if his long nimble fingers were touching me themselves. "Would you make me break my promise?"

Smiling to myself, I walked back through the house to the kitchen. Mercury would come back eventually. He probably just got distracted. He did that sometimes. Phones were a new idea to both of us and while I had to use them on a regular basis Mercury only had me to call.

Residing myself not to worry, I went to work on making myself dinner.

I pulled a wine glass from the cabinet and poured myself a glass of red wine. Finding the radio, I turned it on to my favorite station. Reggae. Kat had teased me for my choice in music, but I enjoyed the offbeat rhythms and chords played by the guitars. The slower pace of it was so much less harsh than the pop rock music Kat seemed to enjoy.

My hips swaying to the beat, I found a frozen premade dinner in the ice box. Reading the instructions quickly before popping it into the microwave oven, I set the timer by what it said on the box. Drinking from my glass, I danced around the kitchen to the beat while I waited for my meal to finish.

By the time, my meal was ready, I'd already finished another glass. If I had been human, I would have stopped at the one glass, especially after drinking at Kat's house, but human wine was nothing like Fairy Tears, the drink of choice in the Underground. I poured myself another glass and sat down to my tasteless meal of some questionable meat and potatoes.

While I had acquired magical abilities in my time in the Underground or what I had called Wonderland when I was a child, I unfortunately never developed the ability to cook. Magical food wasn't something you could just make appear out of nowhere in the human realm. It had to come from somewhere.

I leaned back and sighed, my plate empty as well as my wine glass.

Mercury was still not home yet.

Forcing myself not to panic, I washed my dishes and then took a bath. The plumbing had made leaps and bounds since my time.

Since servants were only something the rich had in this world, I was ecstatic to learn I didn't have to haul the water in myself. I could also have as many hot baths as I wanted without having to worry about my water going cold.

I took advantage of that aspect and laid about in the bathtub until my fingers and toes were wrinkly. Smiling at them and how much my mother would have disapproved, I climbed out of the bath. Wrapping a towel around myself, I tilted my head to the side and listened.

Nothing.

Now, I was beginning to worry.

Where could he be? It wasn't like him to be gone this long without a note or anything to let me know where he had gone.

Finally, I couldn't take it anymore. I grabbed my phone and pressed the shortcut on my screen to dial Mercury. The phone rang and then after a moment a responding ring echoed through the house. With a huff of annoyance, I marched through the house following the sound.

I found it in the living room, stuffed in between the couch cushions.

"What's the point of having a phone if you do not bring it with you?" I growled to an empty room. When it didn't respond back, I went back to our bedroom and proceeded to get ready for bed. If he didn't show up by morning, then I would call Kat.

I would not be that woman who had to know where her lover was every moment of the day. Besides, there was surely a perfectly rational explanation for his disappearance. Perfectly, normal.

A thumping sound made me shoot up out of bed. The room was dark, and the shades were pulled down leaving no moonlight to see by. Another thump sounded. This time followed by a grunt of pain.

"Mercury?" I called out into the darkness, sitting up further in bed.

"Yes, love. It's me." Mercury's shadowy form moved through the room. The bed dipped on the other side and I shifted toward him.

"Where have you been?" Exasperation and relief filled my voice as I reached for him. My fingers found the edge of his long hair before touching his bare chest.

His arms wrapped around me, pulling me close so I could inhale him. The sickly-sweet smell of the grass he smoked, and tea leaves filled my senses and settled my anxious heart. Mercury stroked my hair and murmured reassurances in my ear.

"I apologize, little one." His nose brushed along my forehead. "I thought I would be back before you came home."

"Where were you?" I asked once more, leaning back from him wishing to see his face. The lights next to the bed flared to life. Silvery depth, the color of his very name, bore into me in his sharp angled face. Hair just as silver as his eyes fell over his shoulders and across his naked chest. He only wore a pair of plain black cotton pants, allowing me to look my fill of his pale muscular chest and stomach.

He stroked the side of my face, a small smile on his lips. There was a light in his eyes I hadn't seen since the first time we met back in the Underground. When he used to drink too much tea and he was surrounded by some disreputable creatures. I had wondered if I would ever see that side of him again. It seemed now I would.

"I think I found it."

My brows furrowed. "Found what?"

Excitement lit his eyes and he grabbed both sides of my face. "What's been missing."

Still not sure what he was talking about, I decided to play along a little longer. "And what would that be, dear?"

Mercury dropped his hands from my face and grabbed my hand, placing it against his chest right where his heart would be. "My heart. I think I found the part that's missing."

I cocked my head to the side. "You mean the part you lost in the Bandersnatch?"

Like myself, Mercury had been imprisoned by the Seelie Queen for his part in the incident that led to Moradoc getting free and the death of Kat's former life. While I had been locked away in the Hall of Mirrors to be forgotten, Mercury had gotten the better end of the deal, at least to some.

He'd never told me exactly what it was like to be locked in the Bandersnatch, an alternate dimension ruled by four spirits of the Underground. I knew enough about it from Kat's experience there to know that it was quite easy to lose one's self inside of it. I'd always assumed that had been what happened to Mercury. Why he had changed from being such a lively and passionate Fae to what he was now.

Not that I didn't love this version of his as much as the last, but I would love to see Mercury dance again. To see him smile so brightly that his face matched the color of his red and blue suit. Now, everything was somber and grey. As if the Bandersnatch had leeched the very color from his being.

"Yes," Mercury hissed and then his face fell, and he added, "I mean, no. It's all very complicated and I'd rather not get into it this very moment." His gaze dropped to the clock next to the bed and frowned. "It is quite a lot later than I expected. I didn't mean to be gone so long but you know how the Underground can be. One day could be one hour or even one week. It's hard to tell these days. The hours blur from one right into the next." He smiled again at me expecting me to understand.

I knew what he meant. The Fae world was a tricky mistress. One who didn't play by anyone else's rules. Especially now that so many things have changed. I didn't however understand why he hadn't left me a message at least.

"You forgot your phone," I said instead of hounding him about it.

Mercury's face pinched. "Yes. I did. I realized once I was there, but it was too late to go back. They're getting quite tight on their security as of late. I hardly made it in. It makes one wonder what else may be going on in there." His gaze drifted off to the side and I poked his side, regaining his attention.

Licking my lips, I peered up at him beneath my lashes. "I missed you."

Fingers tipping up my chin, Mercury hummed as he brushed his lips against mine. "As I miss you, every moment of every hour of every day." He took my mouth with his, kissing me until a hot need swept through my entire being.

Mercury may have lost his passion for the rest of life but there was one place he always made up for it.

Had my mother seen me now she would have been appalled that I was living with a man I was not married to, let alone one I bedded. She'd tell me I had ruined myself. Which I never really understood. How could something so deliciously nerve shattering good ruin you? What good was it to be unsullied at all?

"Mercury," I moaned, my head falling back, allowing him access to my neck. "Please."

His lips found the spot between my neck and shoulder and devoured it, nipping, and sucking until I dared not stay on my knees, else I fall.

Laying on my back, Mercury skimmed his hands down my sides, his brows furrowing slightly. "Is this new?"

I shifted on the bed, my gaze dipping down to the small night gown of blue silk and white lace. "Yes, I bought it with Kat the other day. Do you like it?"

There were other outfits Kat had tried to get me to buy. Ones of string and small triangles of fabric that weren't fit to be called lingerie. What was the point of wearing something that showed everything you were hiding?

My pulse raced as Mercury's gaze swept over the small gown. My skin prickled and my nipples hardened under his gaze until they stopped at the top of my thighs. It was the only thing I could stomach actually wearing without feeling completely humiliated. It was all worth it with the way his eyes darkened until they were stormy grey.

"Yes, love," his voice grew husky and deep. "I like it very much."

His hands dipped to my thighs and without asking, I parted them for him allowing the material to ride up and expose my bare core to him.

"Oh, yes. Perfection." Mercury inhaled deeply and a deep rumble came from his chest. He sat between my thighs, pushing them farther apart until I would have been embarrassed to be so exposed to anyone but him. His head dipped down, breathing my scent in, and rubbing his nose along my slit. The first touch of his tongue on my core made my back arch and made a gasp rip from my throat.

"Mercury," I cried out, my fingers tangling into the tresses of his hair. "Please."

He hummed against my center as he continued to make love to me with his mouth. One thing about Mercury was that he didn't leave a job undone. He lapped at my core until my toes curled under and my cries of pleasure were echoing off the walls and the nightstands shook from my magic. Only then did he shift up the bed, pushing his night pants down with him.

I barely had a chance to glimpse his hard length before he sheathed it inside of me.

My eyes rolled back, and I pressed up against him. Mercury's hips rolled against me causing a slow burn that I couldn't abide by.

Gripping his backside with my hands, I pulled him into me further. "Faster."

"No."

My head jerked to either side of the pillow as he continued his torturous pace. "Mercury, please. I cannot...ah...I need..."

"I want to savor you, Alice." Mercury breathed hotly in my ear. "I want to remember you exactly like this, writhing in pleasure, begging me to give you what you need."

"You are a horrible, rotten man."

"I'm Fae, love. It's in my nature." Mercury laughed, causing a vibration through my core and I groaned.

Thankfully, Mercury put me out of my misery and reached between us rubbing his thumb over my sensitive bundle of nerves with sure and firm strokes. Half a dozen of those strokes and I was crying out once more, dragging my nails over Mercury's back and buttocks until blood tinged the air.

He never complained though. A little pain with our pleasure had always been our cup of tea. With how fast we healed it didn't matter either way. The cuts on his skin healed almost faster than I could even make them, leaving any evidence of our love making nonexistent.

When we both fell from our highs, Mercury wrapped his arms around me, pulling me into his chest. His hands stroked my back until my breathing leveled and my eyes grew heavy. His voice was the last thing I heard before I lost consciousness.

"I love you, Alice Liddell."

C H A P T E R

UNEXPECTED GUESTS

THERE WAS AN ODD pressure in the house when I woke. It made my stomach queasy and my eyes tear up. The feeling got worse when I rolled over and found Mercury no longer in the bed with me.

A quick skim of my hand over the mattress found it cold. He'd been gone for hours.

My gaze shot to the nightstand where I'd placed both our phones last night and found them exactly where they were before, meaning Mercury hadn't taken his with him, again.

Flopping back onto the bed with a frustrated growl, I contemplated having to hunt him down today. It so wasn't what I wanted to do and yet it seemed far more enjoyable of an activity than listening to the humans complain even more about the Fae.

A thunk from downstairs made me freeze.

I sniffed the air. It wasn't Mercury. The scent coming from what I believed was the kitchen had a familiar tinge to it, but I couldn't put my finger on it. Lysol and carrots?

A clatter of what had to be pans followed by a cry of pain had me jumping out of the bed. I grabbed my robe off the door hook and wrapped it around me, tying it tight. My feet pounded down the stairs as loudly as possible, not caring if they knew I was coming or not.

Before I even made it to the kitchen, a grumpy voice shouted, "Ye ain't in yer own 'ouse, you louts. Donner touch nothin'."

Recognizing the accented voice, my lips twisted to the side in a grimace. Wonderful. Just what I needed. As if I didn't have enough on my plate as it was.

I stalked into the kitchen, my hands on my hips and scowled down at the two creatures causing such a ruckus. "What are you doing in my kitchen?"

A little brown man in red overalls looked up at me over his bulbous nose, his onyx colored eyes narrowing as he swept the glass up from the floor. "What's it be lookin' like, lassie? We be makin' brekkie."

I frowned at the pans on the stove and the open fridge door with several broken eggs already on the ground. "Yes, I can see that, but why are you doing it in my house?"

"Trip and Mop make breakfast for Bad Lady, yes, we do, we do. Hatter says to keep Bad Lady company, yes he did, he did."

"Donna call 'er that, ye idiot. She's be havin' a name." Mop swatted in Trip's direction making the creature flinch and trip over his own ears.

If I hadn't seen an Opalaught in my time I'd have described the creature that was Trip as a mutated rabbit of sorts. His height brought him to about my waist much bigger than a normal rabbit. His sharp fangs and claws would make anyone nervous just looking at them, but the Opalaught was one of the sweetest creatures in the Underground and wouldn't hurt a faerie. Which was saying something since faeries were a right pain and nobody cared for them.

"Trip," I stepped into the kitchen and bent at the knee, so I was at eye level with the Opalaught. "Did Hatter say where he was going?"

The Opalaught's long tail smacked the ground behind him in a rapid movement, giving off his excitement as he shook his head. "No. No. Hatter no tell Trip or Mop anything. Not anything about where."

I shot a look between the two creatures and pursed my lips before straightening back up. "I need a cup of tea."

"Let me do that, lass." Mop sat the broom to the side and tried to take the tea pot from me. "The humans be makin' piss water fer tea. They donna know how to make it like we fare folks." He winked at me and I sighed in defeat. They were going to pamper and bother me all day, I could already tell.

Wrapping my robe around me tighter, I sat down at the kitchen table. "So, Hatter didn't say anything about where he was going or when he was coming back?"

Trip and Mop exchanged a look. They were thinking about it. Curious. Only Fae who were trying to find a way around a lie thought this hard about their answer. Speaking the truth was sort of code of honor, only those with ill intent tried to lie.

"Look, lass. We canna help ye." Mop placed the kettle on the stove and lit the burner. "Hatter dinna say much. But ye know how he be. Drinkin' too much of his own tea if ye know whatta mean." He shook his head with a sad smile. "Donna know half of what comes outta his mouth or the others." He took his red cap off his head as it dipped down as did Trip's, his ears dragging on the floor. "Only Reaper knows where they be now."

I allowed a moment of silence for our lost comrades before jumping into it once more. "So, what did he say?"

Mop shrugged, turning his back to get teacups.

"Trip knows! Trip knows!" The Opalaught bounced up and down before stopping in front of me. "Hatter says he looks for what's missing. Yes, he does. Yes, he does. What's missing!" He paused for a moment, a crease forming over his brow. "Bad Lady, Alice, not Bad Lady. Not anymore." He giggled nervously and then bounced once more.

"Trip doesn't know what's missing. Can Alice tell Trip what's missing?"

Leaning my face on my hand, I hummed to myself. "Hatter was gone all day yesterday as far as I know but came back saying he knew where it was."

"Where what was? Where what?" Trip asked, his voice shrill enough to hurt my ears.

Mop sat the teacup down on the kitchen table and turned to Trip, smacking him over the head. "What be missin' you, carrot munching imbecile. Now go sit."

Trip didn't argue with Mop and hopped over to the nearest chair. I supposed he was used to his friend's bad temper. It was all very gauche to me. Hitting should be kept for real problems or in the bedroom not for your friends.

I waited for Mop to finish going around the table filling our cups with tea before I spoke. "If I'm to be honest, I do not know exactly what Hatter is missing. Last night, I thought it might be the part of himself he lost in the Bandersnatch but now I'm not so sure." I shook my head and blew on my tea before adding on, "I do not know what has gotten into him lately. It's not like him at all to go off on his own without telling me. Certainly, not leaving me with babysitters."

Mop opened his mouth to argue.

"Do not try to talk your way around that one. I know a babysitter when I see one. Kat did it to me often enough in the beginning. I have only just gotten her to trust me enough to go to the Underground and back on my own without an escort." I huffed and crossed one leg over the other. "As if I could cause any more trouble with the Shadow man gone."

Mop and Trip tensed at the name.

"Ye ain't who ye were before." Mop patted my hand in reassurance. "Ye reformed. Even Trip likes ye now. Doncha Trip?"

Trip nodded eagerly. "Oh, yes. Trip like Alice. Trip like Alice very much. Not the Bad Lady. Not at all."

I smiled politely in return and busied myself drinking my tea.

Hearing them call me the Bad Lady and being reformed ate at my pride. I made mistakes. Of course. Everyone does. However, the circumstances were highly unusual. I was only a girl after all. I only wanted to stay with them forever.

Hatter. I corrected myself. I only wanted to stay with Hatter.

Everything would have been fine had the Seelie Princess not acted like such a whiny ninny. Really, who kills themselves because they see their lover kissing someone else? Talk about dramatic. My mother would have had a field day with that one.

"So," Mop sat his cup down with a clank of china, "what be on yer agenda fer today?"

Lifting my brows, I sipped my tea before answering, "I'm going to see Kat and then I'm going after Hatter. If you would like to tag along, you are welcome to. He did say to keep me company, did he not?"

Mop's mouth dropped open and Trip hid behind his ears.

"But ye canna do that!" Mop finally caught up to himself and dropped his teacup down, tea sloshing over the side. "Hatter wouldna be wantin' ye to go after 'em an' ye know it."

I shrugged a shoulder and stood, giving them the smile I reserved for my worst clients. "Well, we do not know that for certain since he didn't say so. His lack of disclosing his opinion on such an action allows me to do as I see fit. And I have decided I want to find out what he's up to. Now, if you will excuse me. I need to dress."

Sweeping from the room before either of them could argue, I stalked up the stairs. I might not have shown it at the kitchen table but Mercury disappearing this way without a word one way or another about where he was going or how long he would be had me fuming. I couldn't remember the last time I had been so mad.

It took everything I had not to slam the door to my bedroom as I went in. Alone in my room, I closed my eyes and lifted my face to the ceiling. Breath in, one, two, three, four. Breath out, one, two, three, four.

"Get a hold of yourself, Alice." I commanded myself in the mirror. "You are better than this. You're not going to have a panic attack. You are in control of yourself and your future." Feeling a bit more at ease, I took one more deep breath before pushing my magic into my clothes.

Normally, I would have chosen from the array of outfits Kat had made sure I had for my job out of the closet, but I was going back to the Underground. They didn't wear pants suits there. I needed to fit in but be protected.

My robe and nightgown transformed into a blue dress with many layers of white skirts beneath. The skirts landed just below my knees and twirled when I spun around. Thigh high white stockings covered my legs and black with gold buckled shoes sat on my feet. A thick blue corset wrapped around my chest and waist, cinching it tight, but not so much that I could not breath.

My mother would have been so disappointed. Not only for the lack of a tiny waist, but for the fact that I wore my corset on the outside of my clothes rather than inside. I didn't know why I had started wearing it exactly, I only knew that it would protect me. Another thing I lost in the Hall of Mirrors.

Pushing the thought aside, I adjusted the small blue hat on the side of my head and primped the fat curls surrounding my heart shaped face. Lastly, I made sure the kid gloves on my hands were in place before turning for the door.

My hand hadn't more than touched the handle before I stopped and strode over to the bed. Snatching up mine and Mercury's cell phones, I tucked them into a little magical air pocket. Couldn't yell at him for forgetting if I did the same, now could I?

Dressed and ready to go, I marched down the stairs and found Mop and Trip waiting for me in the living room. Trip dragged the fluff on his tail between his paws over and over, his nervous gaze skittering to Mop and back. Mop, on the other hand, had his arms crossed over his chest and a stern frown on his face.

"Ye ain't goin'."

I arched a brow at him. "And who would stop me? You?" I laughed haughtily. "You're nothing but a brownie. You don't have any magic that doesn't involve cleaning." I turned to Trip and smiled gently. "And Trip here wouldn't want to make Alice upset, now would Trip?"

Trip shook his head venomously. "No, Trip wouldn't. No. No."

"Then it's settled." I moved toward the door, the two of them on my heels.

"No, it be not," Mop snipped, putting himself in my way. "Ye donna want to be goin' back down this road, Alice. Ye know what happens when ye go off on ye own."

My eyes narrowed on the little man. "What exactly happens, Mop? Huh?" I placed my hands on my hips and leaned toward him. "Do you think I'm going to make another deal with a malevolent manifestation of dead Fae so that I could be more than human only to put all of the Underground in jeopardy? Is that what you think I will do?"

Mop snorted. "Nah, ye just tend ta stir up trouble where there be none. So, we be escorting ye."

I sighed in irritation. "Fine. Have it your way. Let's go."

A YEAR AGO, WALKING down the street with Mop and Trip at my sides would have gotten me strange looks and people taking photographs. Today, though, I only received a few curious looks, but for the most part no one commented or stared.

We did have to stop a few times. Why they made Opalaughts ears so long and their feet so big was a mystery. I never remembered the March Hare having so many issues tripping over his own ears.

"Do ye have a plan, lass?" Mop grunted as we came into view of Kat's home. "Or will ye just wander aimlessly 'round the Underground like ye did as a child?"

"No, I'm not going to wander around like a child," I sneered back at him. "I do have a half a —"

"Oodle in yer noodle?" Mop filled in for me with a smirk.

A smirking brownie was not something one wishes to see often. It was like watching a carriage crash. It was horrible when it happened and yet you couldn't look away.

"You have spent too much time with Trip." I glanced down at Trip with a small smile. "My apologies."

Mop shrugged. "I donna tolerate many an' I be used to this one." He pointed a thumb at Trip.

"What about Kat?" I asked, making sure to walk extra hard on the front steps and raise my voice. "Do you just tolerate her?"

His onyx colored eyes narrowed on me, his lips pressed tight together. "'Course, I more than tolerate, Kat. She be one of me best friends."

"Ah, Mop. I didn't know you cared so much." Kat leaned against the doorway of the open front door. "So, what brings you all to my doorstep at this god forsaken time of day?"

I arched a brow and glanced at my phone. "It's only nine o'clock."

"Exactly," Kat shot back and handed out a glass of yellow liquid. "Mimosa?"

Rolling my eyes, I ignored her glass and pushed my way inside. "I do not understand how you are the most important person in all of the Underground, and you are drinking before noon. Are you sure you're not an alcoholic?"

"Pfft." Kat downed her glass in one go, letting out a loud gasp at the end. "I haven't stopped drinking and if you had to live with my mother, either of them, you'd drink too."

I sniffed and shrugged. "True."

Mop exchanged a friendly hug with Kat before sitting on the couch.

Trip's greeting was a little different.

"Lady, Lady! Trip has missed Lady so much, Trip has!" The Opalaught wrapped his arms and tail around Kat's leg and hugged her tight.

"I've missed you as well, Trip." Kat patted him on the head softly. "But you know, you just saw me three days ago."

"Trip knows. Trip wishes Trip never had to go back, Trip does! Trip wants to stay here with Lady."

Kat peered down at the Opalaught and then cast a helpless look toward me. I scrambled to find some reason to keep the Opalaught from moving into Kat's home but was coming up blank.

"Good morning all." Chess saved the day by walking into the room with an identical glass as Kat. He was such a bad influence on her. Or was it she on him? I didn't know either way, they were ridiculously in love and it made me a bit nauseous and completely jealous at the same time. Not that Mercury and I weren't in love, but we didn't have the same kind of relationship Kat and Chess had.

"Chess," Kat's relieved voice permeated through the room. "I was wondering when you were going to drag yourself out of bed."

Chess's tail wiped around his ankles, the heat in his eyes still as strong this morning as it was yesterday. "Someone wore me out, any idea who that might be, pet?"

I stepped between their sultry stare down. "Can we focus on the topic at hand?"

"And that is?"

Before I could answer Kat's question, Mop jumped in.

"It ain't nothin' fer ye to worry about. Alice just bein' Alice." He shot me a warning look. "We can handle it. Ain't that right, Trip?"

Trip pulled on his ears and averted his gaze. "Trip and Mop keep Alice company. Hatter said. Hatter said."

Kate glanced between the two of us, frowning.

Crossing my arms over my chest, I narrowed my eyes on the two tricky Fae. "Yes. That's right. Hatter has asked the two of them to accompany me and help me in any way necessary."

Mop glared stubbornly at me.

Chess crossed one leg under the other and leaned against the doorway, not missing a single thing. "Where is dear Hatter?"

I snorted. "That is the question, is it not?"

Kat's eyes widened, her shoulders tense and her jaw tight. "Hatter's missing? How long has he been missing? What do you know? Was there a struggle?" She paused and looked around at us with growing panic. "Well, don't just fucking stand there. We've got to find him!"

Instantly, Chess pushed away from the door frame and came up behind Kat, wrapping his arms around her. "Calm, love. Deep breaths. That's it." He murmured the words in her ears, but they were as clear to me as if he had said them in a normal volume.

It was wonderful how Hatter could so easily calm Kat with just his presence. Kat did have a tendency to overreact so having Chess there definitely made things easier. On the plus side, since they had a heart bond he also knew exactly when she needed it.

I could use something like that, then maybe I would know what Hatter was feeling right now.

With Kat finally not shouting at us, I quickly explained what happened last night and what Hatter had told Mop and Trip this morning.

Kat hummed and cocked her head to the side as she thought. "And he didn't say anything to you about leaving again this morning?"

"No—," I started to say but stopped and frowned as I remembered something. "Though, he was acting a bit odd about savoring me. As if he wanted to remember me?"

Kat wagged her brows at me, a smirking quirk of her lips. "Savoring you, huh?"

I blushed and ducked my head. "Stop it."

Thankfully, she relented on the teaser and sighed. "Fine. You're right. This is hardly the time." Scratching her head and adjusting her ponytail, Kat pondered for a moment. "I honestly couldn't tell you where he went. I mean, you know him better than I do. Where do you think he went?"

Tugging on my gloves, I shook my head. "The only place he could go is the Underground. There is certainly nothing here in the human realm he would want so badly to leave me for."

"Alright then. Let's go." Kat sat down on her couch and dragged her shoes from underneath the coffee table. "We can start at his house and then work our way through." She paused mid-tying of her shoe. "Seer might know something as well. We'd better stop by."

"Love." Chess slid onto the couch next to her. "You can't go with her."

Kat didn't even look up from her shoes. "I know you're not trying to tell me what to do."

A dangerous gleam flickered in her eyes as she smiled at him. "You remember what happened last time."

Chess wiggled on the couch, his tail sliding around her waist. "As delightful that punishment was, pet. I wasn't talking about stopping you. I'm reminding you about your meeting..."

Kat angled her head to the side, frowning. "What meeting?"

Clearing his throat, Chess shot a look toward the others and myself before turning back to Kat. "The one with your parents about the event we wished to discuss."

Mouth forming a u-shape, Kat laid her hands on top of his and turned back to me, an apologetic smile on her face. "I'm sorry Alice, Chess is right. I'd love to come with you, but I have a prior engagement that I cannot get out of."

Curiosity peaked, I asked slowly, "Is there anything I can do?"

"No!" Kat rocked and waved me off with a suspiciously too bright smile. "I mean, no you have enough to worry about. Just keep your mirror on you and let me know if you run into any trouble."

I wasn't nearly satisfied with her answer but knowing Kat, she'd tell me when she was ready.

"Very well." I shifted my weight to one side and placed my hands on my hips. "I suppose I'll have to venture it alone."

"Not hardly." Mop scoffed and shook his little brown head. "Imma not lettin' ye outer me sight. That be Hatter's orders."

I rolled my eyes and scowled. "Since when did you follow anyone's orders but your own?"

Kat stifled a giggle, earning her a glare from Mop.

"That not be true. I followed his majesty's orders well enough." Mop paused and tugged on one of his large ears. "When he be 'round anyhow. Regardless," Mop locked his gaze with mine. "I be feelin' better knowin' you ain't gettin' in trouble."

I huffed. "I do not get into trouble." Everyone stared at me knowingly. "Fine. I attract trouble. However, that is hardly my fault." I placed a gloved hand on my chest. "I'm innocent in all this. I have been taken advantage of. I cannot help that I have a giving heart."

"More like a pain in the ass."

I shot a glower at Kat. "I heard that."

Grinning primly, Kat said, "You were meant to."

Chess slapped his thighs and stood. "I suppose you will be wanting to use the mirror? "

I gave Chess a grateful look. "I would appreciate it. It would be a long walk in these shoes to Kat's grandmother's house. How is she by the way?"

Kat snorted. "Living it up. Ever since the Fae came out of her back yard, she has been hoarded by reporters and talk show hosts wanting to get the low down."

"So, she's loving it?" I countered with a sly look.

She grinned and shrugged. "She's eighty. Grandma hasn't had this much attention thrust onto her since she was my age. Or at least that's what she keeps telling me." Kat chuckled and stood as well. "Come on, I'll shoot her a text letting her know you're coming."

We followed Kat and Chess into the kitchen and then to an office off to the side. A desk sat up against one wall beneath a window which overlooked their garden. I imagined Kat spent many a day manipulating said garden when she couldn't get her mind on her work. A wicker chair overflowing with books had been shoved in the corner next to a tall lamp. The books were of Fae lore from all over the world. I had helped Kat collect them over the last few months. It helped to know what humans already thought of us so we could correct the misconceptions.

"I haven't made much progress," Kat told me, leaning against her desk Chess at her side. "There's far more make believe in the books than fact. Thankfully, not many actually mention our one weakness. Iron."

We all frowned and tensed, visibly uncomfortable from the mere mention of it. There weren't many things that hurt Fae, but iron was one that the human world had in spades.

Changing the subject, I gestured to the full-length mirror on the far wall. "I see you moved it."

Kat's nose wrinkled up. "Yeah, well, after the Fae Council decided to pop in on me one afternoon while Chess and I were having fun times."

Chess smirked and brushed his nose along her shoulder. She shrugged him off with a flick to his nose. "Be good."

Purring deeply, Chess peered up at her innocently. "I'm always good."

Rolling her eyes at him, Kat pushed away from the desk and pointed at the ornate mirror. "Pat's working on finding a way for me to get a warning chime or something before I get a call. In a perfect world I could deny them just like on my cell phone," she shrugged and grinned. "Until then, it stays in the office."

"Understandable. Now can we be gettin' goin'? I got other places to be." Mop shoved passed me to stand before the mirror. He kicked the bottom of the frame making the mirror rock on its axle.

"So impatient." Kat scowled and then smirked. "Got a hot date, do you?"

Mop's tiny arms crossed over his chest. "For ye information, I do."

Kat grabbed her chest in mock surprise. "I'm so disappointed in you. What would your wife say?"

Ears pink, Mop waved her off. "It be with me wife, ye nitwit."

Normally, most Fae wouldn't dream of speaking to Kat in such a manner. Even though half the time she acted more like a toddler than a princess, she was still a scary Fae in her own right. Mop and Kat went way back. When she was a silly human girl without a clue about her Fae heritage.

This, of course, was back when I was still imprisoned in the Hall of Mirrors.

I owed Kat my life.

As did Mop and the rest of the Underground, that was why most of them treated her with respect. Mop treated her like one of his own children. Scolding her when she got out of line and teasing her just as much as she teased him.

"Trip's Petal is waiting too. Yes, Petal is." Trip smacked his tail down on the ground excitedly.

"That is wonderful, Trip. Really it is," I interjected before we got off track again. "But the sooner we get to the Underground, the sooner you can see her. Alright?"

Trip's tail tapped even faster, and I assumed he was consenting.

Turning back to Kat, I gestured to the mirror. "If you don't mind?" Only members of the royal family or those of half-blood, like

Chess, could activate the mirror portals or else all of the Fae would have them in their homes.

"Oh, yeah, sure." Kat scuttled across the floor to the mirror and slid her finger down the side of the frame. Sigils glowed all along the frame until the surface of the mirror rippled.

"Thank you," I stepped up to the mirror and reached out a hand. I have always found going in headfirst to be too nerve wracking and would rather feel where I was going.

The portal felt like cold liquid sliding over my skin. A bit like the gelatin Kat had introduced me to. Not quite liquid or solid. It enveloped me and sucked me into the other side and out into a loud pink flowered living room.

"Oh, hello, Alice. What brings you to my home today?"

THE BETWEEN &
A TOOTHLESS PAIN

KAT'S GRANDMOTHER SAT IN a large overstuffed white and flower printed chair sipping from a teacup, her knitting needles sitting in her lap.

"Ma'am, sorry to drop in on you like this. Kat was supposed to message and let you know I was coming." I rubbed my arms, the feeling of the portal's magic still making my hairs stand on end.

"Oh, dear, ma'am was my mother in law. Just call me grandma." She sipped from her cup and then sat it down on the table next to her. Just as she dipped her hand into the pocket of her bright orange dressing coat, Mop and Trip came fumbling out of the mirror behind me. "Oh, more visitors."

"Stop ye pushin'" Mop shoved at Trip, putting a few feet between them.

I cleared my throat.

Mop's gaze jerked to Kat's grandmother and he flushed. "Oh. Excuse me, ma'am."

"Bah, I'm used to it." She fiddled with her phone for a moment, lowering her glasses so she could see better. "Now, if my granddaughter would actually give me a heads up before using the mirror. Ah!" Her phone buzzed and chimed. "There she is right now. I suppose it's better late than never." She sighed and put her phone down. "Now, where might you be going?"

Trip jumped in before I could answer bouncing all around the living room. "Trip goin' home. Yes, Trip is. Hatter missing. Hatter missing."

"Oh, my!" Kat's grandmother covered her mouth with her hand. "Well, I shouldn't keep you then. It's quite the walk to the entrance. Please do be careful."

I nodded eagerly, heading for the back door.

"And you stay out of my carrots," she shouted after us.

"Carrots? Where are carrots? Trip likes carrots. Trip does."

Mop smacked Trip on the back of the head. "She be talkin' bout ye. Donna touch her carrots."

Trip's ears drooped and his eyes dropped to the ground.

"I have some carrots back at my house. I will give them to you when we get back."

Trip's ears shot up, his tail thumping and he hopped around again, this time knocking the tea pot off the table. It crashed to the ground in a mess of glass and liquid.

"Sorry," I shouted to our hostess. "I will replace that as soon as I return."

"Don't worry about it. I got it at a flea market for a nickel," she called back in return.

I sighed. This was exactly why I ended up on the wrong side of the Seelie Queen. I cared too darn much.

"Let's get goin' before we lose the light," Mop grumbled, taking the front of our little group.

As we walked across the grassy plains, I wondered about Mercury. Did he really expect to find what he was looking for in a single day? Certainly, he would have told me if he planned to be gone longer.

Or maybe not.

Current circumstances told me Mercury wasn't exactly thinking with a full tea pot. I could not assume anything at this point. For all I know, Mercury had done full Wonderland on me. Talking in riddles and speaking in rhyme.

I sighed, my steps a little more forceful than before.

"What be ye problem now?"

Stopping to jerk my heel out of the dirt from where I stomped too hard, I grunted with the effort. "This is all so very ridiculous." I jerked and swung my arms around me. "I thought we were done with adventures. We have a house, a nice tidy income to live on, and friends who actually like us!" I hopped in place and scowled. "But no, he could not be happy with that. He had to go and risk it all!" I stalked over to Mop. "Tell me, please, because I have to know. Am I not enough?" My eyes brimmed with angry tears as I sank to the ground in a heap. "Have I not paid enough for my sins? Is this my punishment?

Give me a tiny taste of happiness and then rip it all away?"

Trip and Mop were silent for a moment before Mop placed a hand on my back. "That not be how it works, Alice. Sometimes things a happen and ye canna blame yer self."

I picked at the grass around me and muttered, "Sometimes I think maybe I'm still in the Hall of Mirrors and this is all some elaborate dream I cooked up to keep myself sane."

Mop slapped me.

My hand went to my cheek as I gaped at him. "What the bloody hell was that for?"

"Stop feelin' sorry fer yer self." Mop plopped his fists on his hips. "The world ain't out to get ya and I ain't gonna be listenin' to yer bitchin' and moanin' the whole way there. Now come on, time's a wastin'."

Not waiting for me to respond, Mop marched away muttering under his breath such obscenities they would make a pirate blush.

Trip sat at my side and I looked down at him. "I'm being quite silly, aren't I?"

The Opalaught's big beady eyes peered up at me.

"Oh, you do not have to say it. I know." I pushed up off the ground and dusted my skirts off. "Sometimes I let my emotions get away from me." I took a deep breath and released it. "Well, you heard him. On we go."

We hurried after Mop into the woods and then to a creek where a cave hid behind a waterfall so small it could hardly be called one at all.

"Mop?" I called into the cave, searching for the brownie. "Hello?"

"Well, donna stand there all day," Mop's voice called out from the dark.

I glanced down at Trip. "Want to hold my hand?"

Trip nodded jerkily and held out his paw. His long claws wrapped around my hand ever so gently so as not to scratch me. Not that it would have mattered. I healed just as fast as someone born as Fae.

Steeling my nerve, I walked into the darkness. The walls glowed with similar sigils to those around Kat's mirror, in a white blue gleam that was almost blinding. It made it easy to follow the lights to where Mop stood at an ominous looking hole.

Grimacing, I bent at the waste. "We really should have a better way of getting in and out of the Underground. I always feel like my mother is tightening my corset again."

Mop arched a black brow at me but didn't comment. He stuck his hand into the hole and just like that the whole three feet of him was sucked inside.

"I guess there's no helping it." I threw my hands up and glanced down at Trip. "Ready?"

"Trip ready. Trip always ready. Hole not so scary. Trip hole much smaller at home. It is. It is. Come, Alice. It's al—" He went up to the hole and stuck his nose in but a bit too far, it sucked him in cutting him off mid-sentence.

Well that was not comforting at all. I was more cowardly than an Opalaught and they were afraid of everything.

"Get it together old girl." I shook my shoulders and straightened my hat. "You can do this. It's not worse than sitting through one of your mother's garden parties." I inched closer, sliding my hand along the edge of the hole. "Just close your eyes and think of England—" my words turned into a scream as my body was sucked into the portal, squeezing me in a million places before spitting me out again.

The hole spit me out into a blindingly white emptiness. Well, not exactly empty. In the middle of the area sat a wooden desk with an up to date laptop on its surface. A two-headed dodo bird used to run the reception desk, but they haven't been for over a year. Now, a more pleasantly looking Fae with emerald hair and pale green skin sat behind the desk, her eyes on the computer in front of her.

Glancing away from the reception desk, my gaze focused on the three other doors before me, one in each direction of the compass, standing on their own in the middle of the white nothing. If one walked past the doors they could walk forever and never get anywhere. That was if they weren't taken by what dwells in the Between.

"Great Pretender," a gruff voice announced, and a tan Fae with golden armor covering every inch of his form stepped forward. His dark brown eyes narrowed on me as his hand touched the hilt of his sword. "We did not have you scheduled for a visit."

My eyes drifted from the guard to the rest of the doors. Where were Mop and Trip? Not seeing my companions, I searched the area. I hadn't been back to the Between in a few weeks, there were quite a few changes since then. More guards for one. "You finally replaced the doors," I pointed out without answering his question.

"Yes, the Moderator requested the doors be replaced. It does our great realm a disservice when the first thing they see is the destruction of the Shadows." His eyes narrowed on me with accusation. "Do you have a pass, Great Pretender?"

"My name is Alice, not Great Pretender," I sneered in return, tired of his contempt. "And I don't need a pass, I am the representative for the Fae and as such can come and go as I please."

"The rules state —"

"Oh, Zed, knock it off," another guard appeared at my side, a smile on his gorgeous face. "We all know very well what the rules say."

The Fae named Zed frowned at the new guard. "But every person Fae or human must have a pass signed by the Moderator and both Queens of the Underground, by law, we cannot let her pass."

"Except for official members of the Court. Miss Liddell is an official member, is she not?"

I watched Zed squirm in place obviously not wanting to admit he was wrong.

"Yes, she is," Zed finally bit out, his jaw tightening as he glowered at me.

"Then get back to your post and stop wasting Miss Liddell's time."

With one more glare in my direction, Zed marched back to the side of the door.

"I didn't know they were being so strict now," I commented in light of thanking him. Thanking Fae had never been a good idea. They tended to see it as owing a favor. I had enough favors I needed to repay already.

"We haven't been, not really. Zed is just a bit...over enthusiastic. I'm Beta. Or I mean, Cedric." Dimples appeared on his cheeks when he smiled. "I keep forgetting we could use our real names now."

I curtsied. "Alice as you know. Pleasure to meet you. I had two companions come through ahead of me, have you seen them?" I glanced around the area and frowned. "One is a brownie who goes by Mop and the other is an Opalaught, Trip. I don't know they're real names." I shrugged apologetically.

Cedric nodded and then pointed toward the door across the way. "They went through the UnSeelie entrance not a few moments ago."

"Oh!" My eyes shot to the UnSeelie door, only discernible from the other doors by the guards standing before it. Instead of humanoid Fae with pointed ears wearing gold armor, there were two Fae of ambiguous origins. There were far too many species of Fae to know all of them by heart.

One of them had pale blue skin and gills on the side of his neck, his black irisless eyes were as dark as his long hair. I could only guess that he was a water nymph of some kind.

The other was significantly larger, fatter as well, with a bulbous nose and big ears. His sharp fangs filled most of his mouth and his beady eyes hungrily ate up everyone in the area. Unlike Mop's red cap and overalls, this one's cap was tinged with blood, the copper scent filling the area. This one, I didn't have to guess on what he was. A Redcap. Nasty creatures. Vicious and untrustworthy. They would eat their own mother if they were hungry enough.

I reminded myself I was the representative of the Fae and a good friend of the Moderator and therefore steeled myself once again. All Fae should respect if not fear me.

I lifted my chin and stalked across the space between the doors. The woman at the reception desk called out to me primly, "Miss, miss you must sign in." I ignored her, my eyes set on the UnSeelie door.

"I wish to enter. Move aside," I pushed as much command into my voice as possible, not wanting to give them a chance to deny me.

The Nymph gave me a half-interested look, leaning on his staff. However, the Redcap sneered and licked his lips as he looked me over.

The Redcap stepped forward and growled, "And who be you to command me?"

Narrowing my eyes on the Redcap, I shoved my finger at his chest. "You should have better manners and recognize your superiors."

Snorting, the Redcap leered over me, trying to intimidate me with the two feet of height he had on me. "You ain't superior to me. Only the Queen be my commander and you ain't she." He reached a sharp clawed hand out and picked up a strand of my hair.

I smacked his hand. "Unhand me, you lout. I am Alice and you will let me pass."

That got the Nymph's attention. He stood at attention and swung out his staff, knocking the Redcap on the back of the head. "Back the fuck up, Barbarous. Or do you want to end up in the Shadow Realm before your time?"

Barbarous spun on the Nymph and clutched the staff between his large hand. "Hit me again and you be dining with the Reaper tonight, Nymph. I don't care who she be. No one command's me, least of all a puny little girl such as her."

Sighing in annoyance, I pushed magic into the palm of my hand and with an invisible force lifted the Redcap by the throat. He growled and gasped as I tightened the hold on his neck. Gurgles came out of his mouth as he tried to fight me off, but I was done with his nonsense.

"Now, you listen, and you listen good, you whiffle-whaffle." Power filled my voice, making it echo in the emptiness. "I do not have time for this. I am the representative, the Great Pretender, Bad Lady, and pain in the ass of all who cross me. If you do not wish to spend your dinner with the Reaper, you *will* let me pass and now."

I dropped the Redcap without warning, knocking him to the ground. A clank of armor from behind me reminded me of my audience. Adjusting my gloves, I turned to the golden guards. All but Cedric had unsheathed their weapons, but they weren't about to attack yet. No, of course not. Fae didn't get involved with other Fae squabbles unless they had too. Though, the apprehension on their faces and if I was being honest, fear, told me they wanted to attack me over the Redcap.

Except Cedric. Who smiled brightly at the scene.

Trying my best not to apologize as my mother would have insisted, I placed a smirk on my face. "Sometimes a reminder is in order."

"Of course," Cedric answered, and then turned to the others. "Get back to your posts. Nothing to see here."

Spinning back on my heel, I stepped over the still gasping Redcap and walked through the door the Nymph had opened for me. I nodded my approval before the magic of the portal sucked me inside and out the other end.

This time I stopped myself in time and flew onto the stone floor, catching myself with my hands. Hissing, I shook them until the burning marks healed. I pushed magic into my hands, repairing my gloves instantly.

"Took ye long enough." Two small red booted feet appeared beneath my face. "It already be dusk. I donna about ye but I donna fancy walkin' 'round in this maze in the dark."

Groaning, I pushed myself up onto my knees and then my feet. Brushing my hands off on my dress, I scanned around us. It was as if nothing had changed.

Tall stone walls surrounded the small alcove we had fallen into. A quick turnaround showed the leave-less tree with a hole the same size as the one on the other side, sitting beside a small pool. I stepped back from the pool automatically. Even being Fae myself, there were creatures in the Underground that didn't care who you were as long as they got their meal.

Turning on my heel, I followed the sound of Trip's hopping until I rounded the corner and saw the two of them making their way down the long never-ending path. They had no thoughts of waiting for me, so it seemed. Not that I blamed them. The sky was darkening, and even worse creatures came out at nighttime. I would hate to be caught here all alone.

"This is not the way to Hatter's house," I commented once I caught up with them. "Should we not go the other way?"

Mop waved me off. "Bah. This way be faster."

"I do not think it is."

"Yes, Alice. Yes. Teeth will let us cut through yes, he will. He will!"

I smiled down at Trip and then frowned at his words. "Teeth? You mean that peculiar wall thing with an obsession with biscuits?"

"Yes," Mop answered, not stopping once.

"The same wall that would likely eat us as let us pass?" I pushed once more, anxiety running through my form.

Mop shrugged. "He hadna eatin' me yet."

Grabbing him by the shoulder, I jerked him to a stop. "That doesn't mean he might not today. I do not know about you, but I like my head exactly where it is. On my shoulders!"

"I thought ye wantin' to find Hatter and quick?" Mop arched a brow at me, causing me to huff.

"I do but not at the cost of my own life." I squinted as I glanced around for another way out. "Is there not another way through the labyrinth without resorting to paying favors?"

"Ye been in the human realm too long, lass." Mop wagged a small chubby finger at me. "Ye know nothin' comes fer free 'ere. Ye pay the favor or ye go it alone. That be the rules."

Huffing, I crossed my arms and muttered, "Fuck the rules."

Mop's brows rose and then he burst out laughing.

"I do not see how it is funny?" I dropped my arms and stomped my foot.

Wagging his finger at me even more, Mop said through his laughter, "And ye certainly been hangin' 'round Kat far too much. Come on, let's be off."

Not allowing me to argue further, Mop began to walk again. I reluctantly followed after him.

I could get through the Underground on my own. I had done it before and that was only being human. Though now even with Fae powers, I felt a strange sort of electricity in the air. Something had changed since I'd last been in the Underground. The walls vibrated with it.

"Are we almost there?" I swallowed thickly and stared up at the sky as it turned dark before my eyes.

"Hold yer horses." Mop stopped abruptly and searched his pockets. "I know I be havin' it somewhere. Ah, there it be!" He pulled a shiny key from his pocket and walked up to one of the walls surrounding us. Red furry moss covered the wall and eyeballs buried into them stared at us in wonder.

Mop tickled one section of the wall and a hole appeared. He inserted the key into the hole and turned it. The wall gave way to an opening, dark and not at all suspicious.

Shoving the key back into his pocket, Mop walked into the room with his head high. I didn't like how unworried he was about all this. Trip apparently felt the same way because he hopped in after Mop like we were going on holiday or something.

I glanced around the area one more time before taking a deep breath and walking into the opening. The ground which had been hard and solid sunk beneath my feet almost making me lose my balance as I became adjusted to the strange consistency.

"Ugh." I groaned, pulling my hand away from the wall I had grabbed for balance. From top to bottom it looked like we'd walked into someone's mouth and it was just one giant tongue. Pink and red colored muscle lined the walls and floor, strange vein-like pieces rippled as we stepped. My stomach rolled and I tried my best to keep the bile down. It would not do to throw up in someone else's body. Certainly not one that might eat me at any moment.

"It not be that bad, lass." Mop glanced over his shoulder with a condescending tone. "Ye live with Hatter and I be knowin' him longer than ye. He be doin' a lot stranger things than this, eh?"

I plugged my nose at the pungent smell coming upon us and mumbled through my closed lips, "Not like this."

Now it was Mop whose nose curled up with disgust. He froze in his tracks and peered deeply ahead to the other side of the room. Whatever it was he saw had not been good because he broke out in a run. Or what he called a run, he was more of a toddler with his short legs and pudgy body.

Trip and I hurried after him, the stench became worse the further we went. Finally, we stopped before a gaping hole in the wall. Here, the muscle had turned grey like meat that was on the turn. Little flies buzzed around what had once been the great Teeth.

"I have never met Teeth, but I do not believe he is supposed to look like that." I pointed at the slits that were not much more than gaping holes instead of eyes. The sharpened points of the larger hole were not so menacing as it might have been had Teeth been alive and well with a good size chunk missing from here and there.

"No. No. No." Mop shook his head back and forth, his hands on his face. "This ain't right at all. I just saw 'em the day before last. He be fine then!"

I stepped closer to the greyed muscle and even went so far as to poke at the side of what I thought might be his face. Nothing. No flicker of life. No anything.

"What could have done this?" I wondered aloud, quickly stepping back from the creature. "And why is it only on this side of his body and not the rest of the room."

"It's the sickness, it is!" Trip grabbed his ears and pulled them over his head with a whine.

"Knock it off!" Mop glared at Trip. "Ye be overreactin'"

"The sickness?" I arched a brow and cocked my head to the side. "I have never heard of such a thing here."

"That be 'cause there ain't no such thing." Mop shot another warning look at the quaking Trip. "Not in a long time in any case." Shifting around, he pulled his hat off his head and closed his eyes.

I waited for him to finish paying his respects before asking, "Then how do you know it is not what is causing this?" I gestured to the grey wall, covering my mouth and nose when I took too big of an inhale.

"I donna know." Mop shoved his hat back onto his head and narrowed his gaze. "But speakin' it into existence wonna do us any good willa it?" Not waiting for my answer, Mop cautiously stepped up to Teeth's gaping mouth and then tiptoed over the entrance. When he was on the other side, he glowered back at us. "Well, come on!"

THE SICKNESS

WHEN WE CAME OUT the other side of Teeth's mouth, I went from gagging to gasping for air. Sickly sweet smoke clouded the entire area, making it impossible to see anything.

"Mop!" I called out, coughing and waving a hand in front of my face as I squinted into the pale blue smoke. "Where are you?"

"Over here, lass." Mop answered a short way away.

I walked in the direction of his voice until I ran into something hard. "Oh, criminy." I grabbed my foot and held it until the throbbing subsided. Walking more cautiously this time, I called out his name once more.

"Will ye hurry it up?" Mop growled, annoyance filling his voice.

"I would if I could see a darn thing in all this smoke." I coughed once more and stumbled once more.

"Trip hold Alice hand. Yes, Trip will!"

"Oh, thank you, Trip." I barely got the words out before his clawed paw wrapped around mine and he was dragging me in the opposite direction of Mop's voice. "Wait, I do not think this is the right way."

"Alice, trust Trip. Alice do!" His claw tightened further onto my hand until I winced with pain. Realizing something was wrong, I tried to jerk my hand from his grasp, but he held on tight. "Alice, come. Yes, Alice does!"

"Let go. Let go of me this instant." I shoved power into my hand causing a little zing of electricity. The creature or whatever it was pretending to be Trip let go of me instantly with a howl and scurried away. "Serves you right. I will not be your meal today."

I stayed where I was for a moment, making sure the creature was not going to come back for revenge before turning back to the smoke covered area. "This will not do at all." Gathering my cheeks, I pushed power through my mouth and out into the smoke. Instantly, the smoke cleared around me. I walked until I hit another wall of smoke and did the same thing as before until I was all the way out of the thickest part.

Now that I could see around me, I was not any happier with the location. Small and large mushrooms of all different neon colors surrounded me. Unlike normal mushrooms these had bumps along the stalks in the shape of a mouth and eyes. As I passed by, little families of them seemed to be judging me with their mushroomy eyes.

"There ye be!" Mop appeared around a bend. "We be waitin' for ye for hours."

I frowned. "I haven't been gone for that long, surely."

Mop rolled his eyes. "'Course not. Ye need to forget 'bout the rules of the human world. Or did ye forget all about the Underground in prison?"

I huffed and followed after him.

My imprisonment was a sensitive subject for me. I had lost a lot of things. Quite a lot of memories as well. I was lucky to remember my human life as well as Mercury or I would have been completely lost. There was no telling what I could have forgotten in that time.

When I made it around the bend, I groaned and wanted to immediately turn around and go back into the cloud of smoke.

"Ah, there you are, Alice," a sultry voice cooed in my direction, puffing smoke from her long pipe.

Trip and Mop sat on small mushrooms at the base of a larger blue one. Lounging across the top of the mushroom completely unbothered by her partial nudity was Seer. Pale blue skin stretched across her body until it reached her six arms where it faded out into white palms. One of those hands held her pipe. Another slid through her periwinkle hair while a third played with the multiple necklaces hanging around her neck.

"Hello, Seer," I forced out my lips, painfully pulling up into a smile. "What an unexpected surprise."

She threw her head back and laughed, the sound coming out raspy and far sexier than it should have been. Seer shifted a leg out from underneath her skirt, letting it dangle over the edge of the mushroom. "Do not bother playing your words with me, Alice. We both know you do not enjoy my presence." She hummed and skimmed her eyes over my form. "Though, I do wish you would reconsider. I can be very handy." She wiggled all six of her hands as well as her brows, her dark lashes fluttering over her obsidian eyes.

Suppressing the urge to shudder, I focused on something else. "Where are your wings?"

Seer's face dropped. She placed the tip of her pipe in her mouth and took a deep inhale before answering, "I am coming to the end of this cycle. My lovely wings have perished as will I in the next fortnight."

Trip squeaked. "It's the sickness! It is! It is!" He dragged his ears around his head even firmer than before, trying to curl himself up into a ball.

"Stop it, will ye? It ain't be the sickness." Mop gestured violently in Seer's direction. "She be cocooning, ye yellow belly eggy melt!"

"Actually," Seer purred and sighed, "The Opalaught is correct."

"What?" Mop and I cried out at the same time.

Curling up around the tube of her pipe, she let her hands splay out over the surface of the mushroom. "The sickness spreads through the Underground once more. None are spared and all will mourn."

"Teeth be taken already," Mop lowered his head in sadness.

"But why?" I asked, not understanding any of this. "What is the sickness? Where does it come from? How do we stop it?"

Seer sucked in and blew out a cloud of smoke, her eyes turning glassy, staring off into the distance. Shadows began to take shape inside the cloud, forming a man with a crown. "More than a thousand years has passed since the High King sat on the Underground throne." The cloud shifted and changed into a large tree. My stomach sank as recognition came to me. The Tree of Life. "With the Tree of Life dead, the Underground can no longer sustain itself."

"So what?" My brows furrowed. "The Underground is feeding off the Fae?"

"Precisely, Miss Liddell." Seer blew another puff of smoke into the cloud, shifting the scene. "One by one the Fae will fall until one takes the mantle or the Tree of Life is reborn." People and creatures fell across the cloud until all was dark.

"How long ye have?" Mop asked, a wavering in his voice.

"The more broken the being the quicker it takes them. I was already in the beginning stages of my next metamorphosis when it took me." Seer sighed lazily. "The Underground is more aware than you realize and will take those it can roll easily. Myself included."

My stomach dropped out my butt. "Hatter."

Her lips quirked up as she nodded her head, her eyes clearing to look at me. "You are much quicker than you used to be."

"What 'bout Hatter?" Mop's dark eyes bounced between Seer and me.

My head hanging to hide my welling up eyes, I breathed out slowly, "Hatter has not been complete since the Bandersnatch. He would be far more vulnerable than even Trip."

Trip peeked up from his ears, his lower lip pushing out into a pout as he whined.

I pushed my tears back and sucked in a breath. "Fine. What can we do?"

Seer shrugged a shoulder, lazily twisting her hand around. "Leave. Only those who are in the Underground are susceptible to the sickness. I am too far gone, leaving would not do me any good, but you can still escape it."

It was tempting. The self-preservation part of me wanted to do exactly as Seer said. Turning tail and running back to the human realm, leaving the rest of them to fend for themselves. Then there was Mercury. I could not leave him behind. Even though he technically put himself in danger without telling me anything and it would serve him right if he ended up getting the sickness because of it.

And yet...I loved him. The very idea of leaving him behind and facing the world alone made me want to curl up into a ball and die.

Damn it to the Reaper and back. Why did I have to be so soft-hearted?

"We cannot leave." I placed my fists on my hips and stared firmly at Seer. "What can we do to stop the sickness from spreading?"

"She already told us, lass." Mop twisted his hat in his hands before shoving it back on his head. "We be havin' to find a new High King or bring the Tree of Life back ter life."

I laughed bitterly. "As if those two things are not the most impossible things."

"As is a human who wished to be Fae dooming us all," Seer pointed out with her pipe. "The Underground is full of impossible things. Why should this one be any different?"

With that, she laid her head down on the mushroom and closed her eyes. For a moment, I thought she might be dead but then she began to snore.

"Alright, then." I turned to Mop and Trip. "Which one do you think will be easier? Finding a new High King or reviving the Tree of Life?"

Mop arched a brow. "Well, seein' as how the Shadow Man sucked the life from the Tree of Life, I donna see how we can be bringin' it back."

"Okay." I sighed, throwing up my hands. "Then who should be High King? What exactly is a High King?"

"Oh, Trip knows! Trip knows!" Trip finally peeked out of his ears, perking up. "The High King is King of all Underground. UnSeelie and Seelie. Yes, he is. Yes, he is. High King rule all."

One eye scrunched up as I grimaced, I asked, "Do we really want someone like that? Who would we even trust to do such a job? Dorian has his hands full in the Shadow Realm. Chess might have been a good candidate since he is half Unseelie and half Seelie, but he and Kat are too inseparable. I have a feeling High King requires a lot of time in the Underground."

"That damnable cat donna belong on a throne of his own makin' let alone the High King chair," Mop snapped with a scowl. "Never mention this to 'em. Never."

Holding my hands up, I took a step back. "Message received. I will never speak of it again. That still doesn't solve our problem."

Mop sighed and scrubbed behind his ear. "I donna know, lass. Let's think on it. Until then, we still need to be findin' Hatter." Seer snored even louder, muttering in her sleep. "Which we willa not do standin' 'round here."

"Where to next? The Tundrey Woods?" I chewed on my thumb as I thought. "I do not know where else to look besides Hatter's house." I paused, my eyes widening. "You do not think he would go back into the Bandersnatch, do you?"

Shrugging, Mop walked toward the exit of Seer's home. "Who knows. Hatter be workin' by Hatter's rules. We just be goin' along for the ride."

I didn't know what Mop was saying but it made sense. Which in itself was scary. My trip to the Underground had just become a bit more complicated. Not only did I have to save my lover but the whole Underground. Why did everything come on my shoulders? I already played the hero once. My time is done. I was retired. Done. Put out to pasture. I thought I had my happy ending. I didn't need another one.

And yet...in the words of Kat. What the fuck, man?

THE TUNDREY FOREST WASN'T like any other forest I'd ever been in. The trees whispered as you walked by and creatures called to you, trying to get you to leave the path. It was here that I first met my Mercury. I'd been lost in the woods with no idea of where to go when I came upon his party of tea drinkers.

The March Hare, Trip's cousin and Hatter's confidant, had quite a temper and if you didn't watch what you said, you were more likely than not to get a teacup to the head.

The Door Mouse wasn't much better though, he was the more disturbing of the troop with the little red door on his chest. He liked to open it and scratch his innards on the regular.

My favorite, of course, was Twinkle. A dog-sized bat with wings that were almost an exact replica of the night sky. He was always so sweet to me.

My heart warmed at the memory but soon grew cold as I knew the empty table that would greet us. There would be no party. No teacups thrown. No innards scratched. Only a sad and lonely table with hopefully, Mercury sitting in the head chair or in his twisted house.

"What are ye goin' to 'em once we find 'em?" Mop asked out of the blue as we walked through the rest of the mushroom city. The night had turned to day as we left Seer behind, making the path a lot easier to follow.

I stared straight ahead, contemplating what I would say. I hadn't gotten so far as to know what I would do to bring him back. If I knew my Hatter, there wasn't anything I could say to bring him back when he had his mind set on something. If he was determined enough to leave me without saying a word then he might not be willing to listen to reason.

Sighing, I shrugged a shoulder. "What can I do? He won't come back until he finds what he thinks he's missing. I suppose I'll just have to go along with him until he finds it."

"Mop and Trip will help, yes Mop and Trip will!" Trip bounced around in my path, making me smile slightly.

"As he said, we be here to help ye anyway. The faster we be findin' what Hatter's missin' the sooner we can all be goin' home."

Hopefully before the sickness takes us all.

None of us said it, but it didn't need to be said.

Before I could say any more on the matter, we came up onto the end of the mushroom city and across a mossy bank.

I frowned. "Uh, where's the Tundry Forest?"

My gaze swept back and forth over the large expansion of swamp that now took the place of the luxurious, yet mysterious woods. A fog rolled over the top of the water making it impossible to see what could lay beneath the murky depths.

Mop stared at the water with a dumbfounded expression while Trip tiptoed to the edge, the ground making squishing noises with each step of his large feet.

"Well, damn it all to the Reaper and back." Mop grabbed his cap from his head and scratched beneath. "This not be here before."

"Could it be part of the sickness?" I mused aloud. "Did it eat the woods?" My heart jumped into my throat. "What about Hatter? If he was in there and now he's —"

"Donna be talkin' nonsense. He be fine." Mop shoved his cap back on his head and threw a hand toward a broken wood sign. "The woods just moved, that be all. See," he marched over to the sign and brushed off the moss and dirt. "Swamp of the Forgotten."

"Well, that doesn't sound like it has a lot of prospects." I crossed my arms over my stomach and stared across the swamp. "If the swamp is here where did the woods go?"

"Trip don't like it here, no Trip doesn't." The Opalaught clung to my leg, his beady eyes peering up at me.

"Neither do I," I murmured, squinting to see through the thick fog.

"Well," Mop clipped, his small fists on his hips. "We canna be complainin' 'bout what we be givin'. We gotta just deal wit it as we be gettin' it."

I scowled and shook my head. "This is ridiculous. We have a sickness to contend with and Hatter to find and now, the Underground is moving things around. If we don't get some help soon, we're not going to make it out ourselves."

"Allo, out there!" A cheery deep voice called out from the fog.

We turned toward the sound and as if on cue the fog cleared enough for us to see a wooden dock and a beat-up boat of metal and wood. As we walked toward the dock, a large Fae with leathery brown skin and long white tusks stood on the deck of the boat. He wore a captain's hat on top of his bald head and a white captain's coat. The coat fought to stay closed around the Fae's bulging stomach, its buttons a second away from popping.

I peered at the dock with apprehension. It barely sat above the water, the edges of it getting splashed every time the swamp moved. The wood that made up the dock had rotted in many places and hardly seemed safe to cross.

"'ello," Mop replied as he walked cautiously across the dock. "I be Mop, ye must be Walrus."

Laughing so jolly as his belly jiggled, the Walrus fellow tipped his hat at Mop, his big brown eyes peering curiously at me. "That's me, alright! What're the Moderator's friends doing this far into the UnSeelie Court?"

My head jerked up from the rickety dock. My eyes narrowing on the creature. "How did you know who we are?"

Walrus chuckled once more, a gleam in his eyes as he spoke. "Anyone with half a brain in his noggin' knows who you all are. While I can't say I've ever had the pleasure of meeting any of you, I've heard enough tales of your shenanigans to recognize the brownie and opalaught who align themselves with the crown and the human who would be Fae."

I huffed but Mop spoke before I could argue.

"Yeah, that be us." Mop glanced around the deck of the small boat. "Where be yer partner? I know ye wouldna travel without that no good kelpie. Carpenter come out ye spineless fish!"

For a moment, nothing happened and then a sickly yellow lookin' Fae with gills and fins on the side of his head and neck came stumbling out of the boat's cabin. Most kelpie were the shade of the water they lived in, green or blue but this one's yellowish tinge made my stomach roll.

"What're you hollerin' for?" the kelpie croaked, stumbling until he almost fell overboard.

Walrus reached out and grabbed him by the back of his overalls and hauled him back into the boat. With a sad smile, Walrus held his companion up. "As you can see, Carpenter isn't doing so well these days."

"What happened?" I asked even though I had my suspicions already.

Shrugging a large shoulder, Walrus peered down at his sick friend. "We don't know. He just started feeling bad the other day and hasn't been the same since. And we don't ever get sick. Sea life has hardened us." He beat on his stomach with a proud grunt.

Trip cried out and pulled on his ears as he whispered to me, "The sickness. It is the sickness it is!"

I glanced down at Trip a moment and then over to Mop who gave me a little nod. Slowly, I inched across the dock, each creak and groan making my stomach drop into my butt.

I didn't fancy getting wet today though it seemed that I didn't have much of a choice in the matter.

Once I arrived at the end of the dock where I could see Walrus more clearly, I explained in a calm and even manner, "We know what's wrong with Carpenter."

Walrus's eyes widened but then his mouth twisted to the side suspicion filling his gaze. "What did you do this time, pretender?"

I let out an indigent sound, shoving my fists on my hips. "Why do you automatically assume I did something?"

Snorting, Walrus stared down at me intently. "Are you saying you didn't?"

"Of course not. I haven't even been in the Underground for months." I dropped my arms down to my sides and stared back at him. I would not be intimidated by some blubber bellied Fae.

"That don't mean nothing. You could have done something in the human world to affect our world. What is it? Just come out and say it already. Then we can fix your mess."

"My mess?" I screeched, stomping my foot, causing the deck to groan underneath me in protest.

"Would ye two knock it off?" Mop scowled. "Yer arguin' ain't gonna solve nothin'. Poor Carpenter be barely holdin' on by a thread as it be." He gestured roughly at the practically comatose kelpie.

Glaring at each other, neither myself or Walrus wanted to give in first. Finally, Walrus dropped his gaze to his friend and frowned. "If you can help him, do it."

I sighed and relaxed slightly. "We can't. Not yet anyway." Then remembering my purpose there, I asked, "Have you seen Hatter?"

Walrus frowned and scratched his chin. "Nope, haven't seen that nutter for a fortnight."

"A fortnight?" I practically screeched. "He just left this morning! Oh, we're so behind."

"Donna worry, Alice. We find 'em."

"Is Hatter missing?" Walrus asked, glancing between us. "Does he have something to do with this sickness?"

I shifted in place. "In a way."

"Then why are we wasting time. What do you need?" Walrus stomped across the deck of his boat over to the gangway, making it rock from side to side.

"The sickness has returned to the Underground," I answered, not believing it myself even after seeing it. "We have to find someone to stop it."

"Then sickness?" Walrus stopped in his tracks, the plank in his hands. "Are you sure?"

Nodding soberly, Mop replied, "Ye should see Seer, she be knockin' on the Reaper's door right now."

"Seer?" Walrus swore and shook his head, his fat folds on his face making a slapping noise with the movement. "Get on, I'll get you across the swamp."

He lowered the ramp onto the dock, making the wood splinter and protest. I barely waited until the ramp was settled before hopping onto it, more than ready to be off the rickety dock. Mop and Trip hurried after me and onto the boat.

I waited for Walrus to pull the ramp back up before asking him, "Where exactly does this swamp end at?"

Walrus shrugged a large shoulder. "No telling these days. We were on the other side of the Orchard right up against the Seelie Crystal Forest. Next thing we know we're looking at mushrooms for days."

Sighing, I found a seat against the side of the boat and then grimaced as my skirts got wet. So much for staying dry. On other matters, this was all getting so complicated. I just wanted to find Mercury and go home. I didn't sign up to be the savior of the Underground. That was Kat's role, not mine. I'd always played on the line of right and wrong, only crossing it the one time. Unfortunately, once was enough because now all of the Underground knew who I was and what I'd done. I didn't think I would ever live it down.

"Alright, then. Everyone ready?" Walrus sauntered over to the cabin and took hold of the steering wheel through the window. After Trip and Mop found their seats, we all called our consent before Walrus shouted, "Anchors away!"

The boat jerked to a start and we were on the move—the anchor cranking up on its own as we pulled away. The water slogged around us, the ride bumpy and not at all pleasant. Each time we jostled, swampy water splashed over the side and drenched my backside even more than before. At this rate, I'd be completely soaked by the end of the trip.

We were mostly quiet the whole ride, the bumpiness of the ride making more than just me a bit green around the gills. Carpenter laid on the top of the deck not bothered by the way the boat swayed from one side to the other. Though, I didn't think much of anything would bother him the way he was out cold. Not even Walrus's off-key singing seemed to knock him out of it.

"How much longer?" I groaned, getting up onto my knees to peer over the side of the boat. I couldn't see anything ahead of us through the fog. How Walrus could see where we are even going was beyond me.

"We're about halfway," Walrus called over his shoulder before resuming his singing.

Letting out a long moan of annoyance, I flopped back down onto the deck.

The whole boat shook.

"Geez, Alice. Donna wanna be throwin' us all overboard do ye?" Mop complained from where he sat curled up in a ball.

Huffing, I snapped, "That wasn't me."

"Then who else be shakin' the boat?" Mop snapped back then grabbed onto the side of the boat as it shook even harder.

"Walrus," I yelled, then squealed as the boat almost tipped on its side. "What's going on?"

"Sirens!" Walrus shouted, grunting in the effort to hold onto the steering wheel. "Hold on!"

"Sirens?" I squeezed my eyes shut as water splashed over the side. "I thought they only lived in the ocean?"

"Not anymore," Walrus replied.

"Mop," I drew out, reaching for the brownie. "What do we do? Sirens eat anyone who falls in their waters, right?'

Mop was quiet for a long moment and then said, "Usually..."

"Don't you worry," Walrus called out, "I have it all under control."

The boat got hit once more, this one throwing Trip and Mop into the air. Thinking quickly, I pushed power into my hands and grabbed them from the air, pulling them back toward the boat.

"Thank ye, Alice." Mop gasped, visibly shaken.

Trip clung to me so hard his claw dug into my flesh.

"We can't just sit here," I grumbled and slowly pushed to my feet. "We don't have time to be someone's lunch." My stomach growled at the words. I hadn't had breakfast let alone lunch yet but food later, survive now.

Moving slowly to the middle of the boat, I tried to use my magic to level out the vessel. To my dismay the sirens were stronger than I expected, knocking me onto my knees. "Walrus, can't we go any faster?"

"You got it, Pretender!"

I gritted my teeth against responding to his insult and pushed even more power into keeping us afloat. I'd never met a siren but from what I'd heard they were flesh eaters and would usually draw their prey in with their siren song. They seemed to be skipping the singing and going right for the feed now.

"We're almost there!" Walrus called to me and I sagged in relief.

Of course, nothing goes as planned in the Underground. The moment I let my guard down the sirens hit the boat with a massive attack and I couldn't hold it. The boat shattered beneath us, the waves shoving us up and into the air.

Mid-air I searched for Mop and Trip. Once I found them, I shoved my power in their direction pushing them up and away from the water toward the shore. Walrus and

Carpenter were out of my sight before I could grab them and then I was crashing into the water. I barely had a moment to hold my breath before I went under.

The murky water made it impossible to see anything around me so I swam as fast as I could up toward where I hoped the surface was located. I hit the surface and gasped for air just before something latched onto my leg and dragged me back under.

Kicking my feet at the siren, I tried to dislodge myself from her. Trying to aim in this mess was near impossible and before I knew it, I was being dragged further and further away from the surface. My lungs burned and my eyes grew heavy.

I had to get out of here. They were waiting for me. Four murky figures flashed in my mind and I reached for the thought but the more I grabbed for it the more it fell away until all that was left was pain and the coldness of the water.

C H A P T E R

FUCKING FAERIES

MY CHEST BURNED AND something kept hitting it. This wasn't right. If I were dead then I shouldn't feel any pain, right? I'd be a spirit floating around the Shadow Realm or waiting for the Reaper to come collect me. I shouldn't be feeling like I was being squished to death.

"Come on, ye stubborn lass. Breath!"

Mop?

I choked as thick liquid fought up from my lungs and out of my mouth. Groaning, I rolled over and hacked even more water out of my lungs. It tasted like a toilet dipped in garbage.

"Ah, there she be!" Mop called in my ear, patting me hard on the back. "We thought we lost ye."

I waved him off and rubbed at my eyes. "Nothing can keep me down."

Chuckling, Mop knelt beside me. "I figured as much. Yer lucky the Walrus grabbed ye when he did or ye'd be siren food by now."

I blinked rapidly before opening my eyes completely. "Walrus? He saved me?"

"Yes, Walrus did!" Trip hopped around in front of me, his tail smacking the ground and making my ears ring. "Walrus saved Alice, yes Walrus did!"

Searching around the sandy bank, I didn't see anyone but Mop and Trip. "Where did Walrus go? What about Carpenter?"

Mop glanced back toward the swamp. "Walrus be searchin' for Carpenter. But I donna think he be findin' 'em."

"What about the sirens, isn't he worried they'll eat him?" I pushed up onto my elbows and focused on breathing normally. I never wanted to do that again.

"Nah, Walrus be havin' tougher skin than that. Sirens ain't gonna eat him." Mop waved my concern off and then shifted to his feet. "We better be goin' though. It'll be dark again soon."

I stared up at the sky as I allowed Mop and Trip to help me to my feet. "Already? It hardly feels like it was a whole day."

Mop cocked his head to the side and gave me a once over. "Ye might wanna find somethin' else to wear."

My gaze dipped to my clothes and I groaned. I looked like something the cat dragged in from the nasty swamp. The blue of my dress was more of a muddy brown and my stockings were completely ruined. I didn't even want to see what my hair looked like.

"Ugh," I smoothed my hands over my clothes and they instantly cleaned themselves. Sliding my hands through my hair, my wet locks dried and turned back into the soft curls I loved. "That's better." I tapped my foot to make sure I had gotten all the water.

"So," I glanced around us, frowning as I tapped my chin, "where are we now?"

Mop walked away from me over to where the sandy bank turned into dry dust. The fog that covered the Swamp of the Forgotten hit an invisible wall, stopping it from going past its border. A few steps up to where he stood and I could make out some bushes and trees spread out sparingly along a desert wasteland.

"Oh, no." I placed my head into my hand. "Please tell us we're not in —"

"The Veil of the Faeries?" Mop answered for me with a twisted frown. "Unfortunately, that exactly be where we are."

Trip moaned and shook in place. "Trip don't like faeries. No Trip don't."

I looked down at the opalaught and patted him on the head. "Well, you won't find many here, most of them have taken off into the human world." I shook my head and sighed. "I have more faerie complaints than anything else."

Mop grunted. "Well, keep ye eyeballs peeled. Donna be no good to be caught unaware."

Taking hold of Trip's paw, I stepped cautiously out of the fog and into the Veil of the Fairies. The fairies weren't the only thing we have to worry about in the veil. The Veil of the Faeries was also known as the Fae graveyard. The pesky little creatures were supposed to keep the spirits of Fae in the graveyard for the Reaper, who would come by and collect them as he seemed fit.

I'd never met the Reaper myself but Kat had. He didn't seem too bad from the way she described him but then, he was in his world and not in the UnSeelie Court. Here his form wasn't quite so visible, leaving him more of a shrouded shadow than anything.

A collection of giggles echoed through the sky, setting my nerves on end. Fucking Faeries. If there was one creature of the Underground I couldn't stand it was those little creeps.

"Yowch!" Mop squawked and swatted at the air. "Ye nasty bugger, come do that to me face if ye dare! I be havin' ye for lunch!"

Another giggle sounded before a sharp pain pulled at my scalp.

"Ah!" I reached for the spot. Glaring at the darkness, I searched for the tiny little creature. "You better watch it. I'll make sure you never get out of the Underground."

Some chittering came in response that I didn't understand.

"Ye wastin' yer breath on them." Mop frowned and swatted once more at the air but the buzzing creature was too fast. "These donna wanta be in the human realm."

Trip squealed loudly and hopped around as a dozen gray skeletal creatures with veiny twig wings surrounded him, pulling at his tail and long ears.

"Hey! Leave him alone." I whacked at the creatures but they buzzed out of the way before I could hit them. Now they turned their attention on me, chittering and giggling the whole time. Still tired from the last mishap, I had no patience for their nonsense. I gathered my power inside of me and then pushed it out, shoving the faeries several feet away.

"Serves you right," I huffed in satisfaction. "We don't have time for you. We're already far too late."

A chorus of chitters were my response.

Turning to Mop, I asked, "Do you know what they're saying?"

Mop picked at his clothes. "Nothin' nice."

"Have they seen Hatter?"

My question earned me a set of excited chitters followed by one of them pulling on my hair. I spun around to swat at them but the faerie hadn't been trying to hurt me. It wanted me to follow it. Its big black eyes blinked at me as its small mouth chittered while it pointed and gestured for me to come.

"Do you know where Hatter is?" I asked, eagerly following after the faerie.

The faerie led me over to a bush where I pushed back the branches and leaves to see a nest. In the nest laid several other faeries but these weren't in any kind of condition to attack me. The faerie who led me there chittered noisily and pointed at the faeries laying in the nest.

"What's it saying?" I asked over my shoulder to Mop.

Mop stepped up behind me and shook his head. "They havena seen Hatter, lass. They be too busy takin' care of their sick. Seems the sickness ain't bein' pick who it takes."

Frowning at the sight of the usually rambunctious and annoying creatures laying so pathetically at our mercy, I couldn't bring myself not to feel for them. They might be a pain in my arse but no one deserved to go out like this. I had to help them.

Turning to the faerie who had led me there, I told it, "We're working on it. Just keep them safe and comfortable."

The faerie chittered happily before pointing down the long pathway.

"The queen be that way, he be sayin'." Mop took a few steps in that direction.

"Oh." I swallowed and took a step back. "Uh, I don't think we need to bother her. We can figure this out on our own."

Mop arched a brow at me. "Ye canna be scared of facin' 'er forever. Her majesty willa be more worried about the sickness than takin' her ire out on ye."

I squirmed in place and then nodded reluctantly. Mop was right. I couldn't let my fear of the UnSeelie Queen stop me from finding Hatter and saving everyone. Besides, she could have seen him or could give us a shortcut to get to him. I doubted making my life hard was on her agenda today...I hoped.

To my delight my pocket began to yell loudly.

The faeries squealed and grabbed their ears, chittering angrily at me.

Rolling my eyes at them, I walked a few paces away and withdrew my compact mirror. The surface of it rippled and a big blue eyeball stared out at me.

My brow furrowed as I leaned in. "Kat? Is that you?"

"Oh! You are there." Kat backed away from the mirror, allowing me to see her whole face. "Hey, I just wanted to check-in and see how things are going? Your cell phone keeps telling me your phone is busy."

My eyes widened and I dug into my other pocket only to pull out two completely dead phones. "Uh," I chuckled nervously. "I kind of had an accident. The phones won't be working for a while. Do you have a big bag of that rice from before?"

Kat arched a brow. "Did you drop it in the bath again? I told you, learn from my mistakes. Electronics and bathtubs may be tempting but you'll regret it in the long run." She paused and glanced off into the distance. "Except for your vibrator. That's the only exception and only if it's waterproof." Kat shuddered visibly. "No one wants a shocked vagina."

My face heated and I looked away groaning, "Katherine. Please. I'm not alone."

Curious as her namesake, Kat tried to peer around me. "Where are you?"

I shifted around to show her the others. Mop and Trip waved, though Mop's cheeks were pink with embarrassment. I didn't think Trip knew what Kat was talking about thankfully. When the faeries still hanging around saw her, they all got up in the mirror and chittered loudly, some of them even tried to pry it from my hand.

"Hey, knock it off." I swatted at them and pulled the mirror to my chest. "She didn't call to talk to you. Shoo. Shoo."

A few faeries made some very rude gestures as they chittered and flew away.

"Sorry about that," I blew my hair out of my face. "Nasty little buggers."

Kat shrugged. "What can I say? I'm a national treasure, everyone wants a piece of this ass."

I snorted. "If only they knew what a big head was attached to it."

"Hey, I don't have a big head." Kat's hands touched the side of her face and she shifted to the side but before she could get a word out Chess's voice called out, "Your head is fine, kitten. As well as your ass."

Grinning prettily at his answer, Kat turned back to the mirror. "So, what's the big commotion? Why are you in the Veil of the Faeries and why don't I see a very attractive yet solemn Fae with you?"

I sighed and recapped what had happened so far. Kat's face grew less carefree and more serious with each word I said.

When I told her about Seer, she damn near threw the mirror at the wall.

"I'm coming to help, my parents be damned." The mirror got set down somewhere and I heard some shuffling and cursing from Kat. She walked past the mirror but I could only see a fraction of her and then Chess chased after her as she stalked around the room.

"Don't tell me not to go," Kat snapped at Chess, waving a shoe in the mirror's view. "I'm not going to sit here while Fae are dying."

"I'm not telling you to, love," Chess argued, taking the shoe from her with his tail. "I am saying to get all the facts before you go marching off halfcocked."

"Oh, and you would know all about that wouldn't you," she shot back suggestively.

Sighing impatiently, I tapped the mirror's surface. "Hello, still here and Chess is right. You can't come here."

The mirror lifted and Kat's face filled the surface. "Why not? Don't you want my help?"

"Of course, I do. But anyone who comes here will be susceptible to the sickness. I won't risk you." I gave her a stern look. "You're too important to the cause to lose to something like this."

"But I can't just sit here." Kat and the mirror dropped lower. I assumed she sat down.

Shaking my head, I said, "You won't be. You'll be doing your job. If you really want to help, see if you can figure out how to revive the Tree of Life or find someone to take the High King's place."

Kat's nose scrunched up. "Someone to give me orders and make me obey? No, thank you."

Chess made a comment in the background that made Kat's face turn red. "That's different and you know it you pervy cat!"

At least, I knew my friend could actually be embarrassed. She embarrassed the lot of us often enough of the time.

"Either way, pick one and figure it out. I have my hands full as it is over here with the Underground not staying where it's supposed to." I shifted uncomfortably and glanced toward the UnSeelie castle off in the distance. "Now, if you'll excuse me, I have to go talk to your ex-fiancé's mother."

Kat winced. "Good luck. Mab isn't the easiest person to get answers from. However, on the bright side at least it's not my mother!"

I scowled at her image. "That's not comforting at all."

Shrugging a shoulder, Kat said, "Not my problem. Talk to her about her flowers. She likes that. Just..." she made a squinty face. "Don't talk about the roses. She's still a bit sore about me fucking them up last time."

Letting out a puff of air, I nodded before the screen went dark. Turning back to Mop and Trip, I straightened my hat on my head. "Ready?"

THE UNSEELIE QUEEN

THE WALK TO THE UnSeelie palace was as stiff and uncomfortable as one of my mother's garden parties. Trip was the only one who didn't seem bothered by having to go see the UnSeelie Queen. Mop's brows hadn't stopped furrowing since we headed toward the palace but I didn't know if it was because of who we were seeing or the whole sickness problem. Either way it made the walk seem more like a death march than anything.

It wasn't like Mab hated me. Well, not before. She used to like me very much. We played lots of games and even had games together but that was before I got her son cursed and made a mess of everything.

I hadn't actually faced her since the unfortunate event. I feared what I would find on her face when I saw her. Anger? Disappointment? A need for vengeance?

Mab had been more of a mother to me than my own who wanted me to settle down, get married, and stop my silly stories. In her defense, they were fantastical. It wasn't my fault she didn't believe me. Lewis had been the only one who actually seemed interested in them but then again, he was only using me for his stupid book.

My fingers curled into fists as I thought of the man I once was going to marry. What kind of person pretended to court you just to get information for their work? And to think I was in love with that man. A sly satisfied grin slid up my face. But I'd gotten the last laugh.

"I donna like the look on yer face, Alice. What ye be thinkin'?" Mop gave me a sideways look.

I sighed happily. "Oh, just memories. Happy, happy memories."

Raising a brow in my direction, Mop said, "That wasna happy face ye were makin'. It be like those ones Kat be havin' when she be 'bout to do somethin' we be gettin' in trouble fer."

I shrugged. "Can't get in trouble for something in the past, now can you?"

"Not when it be ye," Mop muttered under his breath.

Shooting him the stink eye, I didn't bother to comment. Coming up upon the hedge maze that surrounded the UnSeelie palace, a strange feeling tugged at my chest. I couldn't place it but I felt like something happened here. Something I didn't remember. It was important though.

"What be ye frownin' fer now?"

I skimmed the hedges frowning further before shaking my head. "Nothing. Let's go."

Mop paused for a moment, his eyes boring into my back before he harrumphed and followed after me. Trip had already gone ahead, happy to be out of the Veil of the Faeries and somewhere familiar. What a wonder it must be to have such a childlike outlook on life.

When I was a child the tall walls of the maze had been intimidating but after playing in them for several weeks, I felt more at home there than I had in my own backyard. Now the hedge seemed to loom over me as if judging every step I took. I glared up at the hedges and stepped more purposely along the path.

Trusting Trip to know where he was going, we allowed him to lead us this way and that until he stopped abruptly. A tall Fae with skin so pale he was almost translucent stood in Trip's path. His muscles bulged beneath the shiny black armor he wore, his hand on the hilt of his sword. Bright purple eyes stared down at Trip menacingly before jerking up to Trip and myself.

"Who dares trespass in the queen's garden?" His voice boomed through the air, making the ground shake and Trip cover his face with his ears.

Frowning, I stalked up behind Trip and placed a comforting hand on his head. "Would you pipe down? There's no need to yell."

The guard frowned down at me curiously. "You are trespassing. I do not take orders from you."

"Well, I don't take orders from you either," I countered with a huff. My eyes slid over to

Mop who only shrugged. He was as clueless as I was to this guard's presence. "When did the queen care who came into her garden?"

"Since now." A wicked grin slid up the Fae's face. "I say who does or does not enter the queen's presence. Now, state your business else meet the Reaper."

I tossed my hair over my shoulder and scowled, "I'm surprised you don't know me. Everyone does."

The guard's confidence dropped for a moment before gearing back up. "I do not care who you are. I only know that no one is allowed in the queen's garden without her permission and she has not given anyone permission to be here today."

I glanced up at the sky as it began to lighten once more. "How do you know?"

The guard's brows drew together tight. "What do you mean, how do I know? The queen would tell me herself, of course."

Seeing where I was going with this, Mop stepped in. "Seein' as it be a new day, have ye seen the queen yet to ask 'er?"

Puzzlement covered the guard's face. "Why no? Not yet. But she would have told me about you."

I blinked up innocently at him. "When? While she was sleeping? Certainly, you don't expect the Queen of the UnSeelie Court to drag herself out of bed to tell you someone is coming? We hadn't even known we were coming ourselves until just a few moments ago."

"See," the guard shot back thinking he caught us. "The queen doesn't know you are coming so you do not have her permission."

"But don't we?" I arched a brow. "We wouldn't come if we didn't. Have you asked her?"

"But you just said, she wouldn't..." the guard fumbled over his words clearly having a hard time keeping up with the situation.

"Oh, Vydriel," a low sultry voice crooned. "Have you been bested by a child?"

The guard, Vydriel, straightened abruptly and turned toward the voice coming from behind him. "Your majesty, please forgive me for my insolence. You should cut off my head and toss me to the Reaper for my betrayal."

A haughty laugh filled the air. "I do not think that will be necessary today, Vydriel. Please retire for the day. I will escort my guests into the garden."

Vydriel bowed deeply before walking straight into the hedge where he disappeared without a trace. In his place stood a voluptuous woman with skin the color of the full moon and hair as dark as the night sky. Her ruby red lips curled up into a telling smile as she surveyed us. The black dress she wore made her seem as if she were floating as she moved toward us.

She reached a single pale hand out to cup my face making the black netting of the sleeves spread out like bat wings. The sharp black and white nails sat so close to my eye, I tensed. "Alice," she purred ever so seductive and yet menacing. "I was wondering when you would grace me with your presence."

Swallowing thickly, I opened my mouth to speak but her thumb traced along my bottom lip pulling it down before releasing it. Trying again, I stuttered, "I've been busy in the human —"

"Spare me your excuses," Mab released me abruptly and stepped away, her dark blue eyes dropping down to my companions. "So you accompany this one as well?"

Trip bounced on his heels completely unaware of the underlying message in her words.

Mop pulled his hat from his head, sweat clear on his forehead and he bowed to Mab. "Yes, yer majesty, we be runnin' an errand fer Hatter but seems Hatter be missin'."

Mab's gaze wandered for a moment, a sort of trance like expression on her face. "Ah, yes. He is not the only one who has gone astray." Her hand reached out into the air and then tightened into a fist suddenly. Her lips curled up at the edges as her gaze locked onto mine. "You have risked a lot coming here, Alice. And all for your Hatter."

I dipped my eyes for a moment, my hands unable to stay still at my sides as they grasped and released in my skirts. "There is more at risk now than just my Hatter."

"As I have been informed." She looped her arm into mine and began to walk, forcing me to come with her. "Come, tell me all that has happened since you were released."

"No offense meant, but are you sure there is enough time to be speaking of such things? With the sickness moving so quickly we need to —"

Mab drew to a stop and stared down at me. "I believe I know when such things should be spoken of and when not? Or do you think you know more than a queen?" She brushed my hair away from my face with her free hand. "Well, do you, Alice? Or is it the Great Pretender? It's so hard to keep up these days."

My mouth went dry as I tried to swallow. "Uh, no. Of course not. I just didn't want to bore you, your majesty."

"So formal now, Alice? I once thought of you as a daughter and now you act as if we are naught but strangers?" She began to walk once more paying no mind to if Mop and Trip were following behind. We rounded a corner and came into the center of the hedge maze.

I used the moment of awe at the garden around us to give me a chance to gather my thoughts. It hadn't changed much since the last time I'd been here so many hundreds of years ago. I had missed the long rows of bushes with all kinds of flowers from roses to Hydrangeas in every size and shape. As we walked along the stone path and around the stone fountain the flowers whispered, telling the queen the going ons around the UnSeelie Court.

My gaze shifted to the water fountain. Sitting at least three meters tall, its stone structure depicted a tragic love seen. Two

Fae, one man and one female embraced gazing at each other lovingly in front of a small replica of the Tree of Life. Peering out from behind the tree was another woman, anguish on her face.

The first time I had seen the fountain I had found it beautiful in its tragedy but now it hit too close to home. Swallowing down my guilt and tears, I turned my face away from it.

"It's lovely, isn't it?" Mab interrupted my thoughts. "It was the last High King of the Underground and his lover. Another Fae woman loved him as well but he only had eyes for her."

I inclined my head. "It's very lovely."

Mab gave me a sly sideways glance. "It could also be seen in another way, don't you think?"

Biting back my remark, I allowed her to continue even though I knew the blow was coming.

"Does he love her? Or does he only think that the one in his arms is his love? Perhaps the one behind the tree has walked in on a moment of passion that was not meant to be?" Her hands tightened on my arm until I winced. "What do you think, Alice?"

"I like the first story better," I muttered, not meeting her gaze. Mop and Trip waited behind us, knowing better than to interrupt the queen and me.

Her hands released my arm and she floated around the fountain. "I like it too." Wandering until she walked completely around the fountain, Mab let her fingers trail through the water falling from the spouts. "Tell me, Alice. Do you enjoy your time in the human realm? You were so quick to leave it before. I'm surprised you would want to go back."

Licking my lips, I said, "Much has changed since then. I have friends and a job."

"And Hatter," she added on with a sly smile. "Perhaps you have more here in the Underground than you think? Have you forgotten all your loved ones here as well?" The way she said it was telling. She was trying to tell me something in her roundabout way but I was tired and not in the mood for her games.

"If I have, they haven't reached out to me either," I quipped in return and flipped my head to one side. "I know you want to get reacquainted, but we have been traveling all day and night. Could we have time to reset and perhaps have something to eat before I regale you with my tale?"

Mab pursed her lips before nodding slightly. "Of course, how rude of me to forget my manners. Please, let us retire inside. We will find you something suitable to eat as well as somewhere to rest, and then I hope we can find some time to talk again before you have to be on your way once more."

Refraining from thanking her, I grasped the sides of my skirt and curtsied, "That sounds wonderful, your majesty."

10

I STARED UP AT the canopy of the bed Mab had assigned to me. My eyes were tired but I couldn't get them to close. My mind kept wandering as I ran over the scenarios in my head.

There were too many unknown variables for what could happen next. Not including my talk with Mab that had to be done, I still didn't know where Hatter was or how to stop the sickness. All that has seemed to be accomplished was almost drowning, getting mobbed by the faeries, and now being interrogated by Mab. I was no closer to doing anything I came here to do.

"Oh, Mercury," I murmured to myself, rolling over on the bed, "where are you?"

I awoke from my slumber with a jolt, sitting up straight in the bed. If I dreamed, I didn't remember it. Except I found my legs sliding over the edge of the bed and my feet moving across the floor. I didn't know where I was going, only that I had somewhere to be.

The palace halls were stone and sparingly decorated. Whoever had created the palace had left most of the castle open to the night sky.

Night? Again? I didn't think I'd slept that long and yet time in the Underground had always been a little off. The days you were having fun could last for a week and only feel like a day. While the others, the more horrid times, dragged on for months at a time only to find out it'd only been a few minutes. I had experienced both types of moments in my time in the Underground.

I received a few curious looking from servants who were wandering the halls. The guards hardly gave me a sideways glance as I passed by and into the garden once more. For once Mab wasn't in the garden. I was thankful and didn't question my good fortune as I hurried down the stone path and passed the fountain without a second look.

My feet seemed to know where they were going as I walked into the hedge maze. I let them lead me as they will, turning one way and then the other until I thought I would never stop. When I finally arrived at my destination, I found myself in a large alcove surrounded by hedges. A wooden table with benches sat on one side of the clearing while a blanket laid spread across the ground.

Frowning, I walked over to the table, my fingers trailing over the top. Mumbled speech and laughter echoed in my ears as I reached for a memory. I had been here before but when? I didn't recognize any of the voices in my head except Hatter's. The others were familiar but I didn't know who they belonged to and yet my heart ached.

Glancing away from the table, my eyes burning with tears, I walked over to the blanket.

I stared down at it for a long moment and then tilted my head back to look up at the sky. Had I laid on this blanket watching the stars before?

The wind blew into the alcove and the distinct scent of Hatter and myself, as well as several others, wafted up from the blanket. Kneeling, I placed my hands on the blanket and dipped my head down. No, I hadn't been mistaken. There was a distinct smell of Hatter and me...my face heated, sex. We had sex here as did several others.

That wasn't too strange. Perhaps this was a regular rendezvous place for couples? If no one ever washed the blanket, our scent would have mingled together just as easily. Though, it was a bit disturbing to think of laying on a used blanket.

Pushing back the disgust rising, I allowed myself to sink down to the ground and onto my back. My eyes went to the sky above me and a feeling of nostalgia came over me. Tears built up in my eyes and they slid down the sides of my face before I knew they were even there.

Touching the wetness, I stared at it with wonder. Why was I crying?

"Your mind may forget but your heart," Mab's voice caused me to jerk up to a sitting position wiping at my eyes, "your heart remembers."

I frowned at her. "I don't know what you mean. I haven't forgotten anything." Well, that wasn't completely true. I'd forgotten quite a few things while I was in the Hall of Mirrors but how could I miss what I had forgotten?

Mab hummed but didn't comment on it. Instead, she held a hand out to me, "Come, let us walk."

Hesitating, I slowly lifted my hand into hers. Mab pulled me to my feet with more strength than I expected, making me stumble as I stood upright.

Without speaking further, Mab turned and moved out of the alcove and back into the hedge maze. I followed after her a step behind, not sure what to expect from her. She's what the talk show hosts called a wild card. One moment Mab was my best friend and the next, she wanted my head on a platter. The only one who was worse than her was her cousin, the Queen of the Seelie Court, Kat's mother. I counted my blessings that my friend was nothing like her mother or I'd have probably killed her and myself long ago.

Mab didn't speak until we reached the end of the hedge maze and the Orchard's trees were peeking into view. "You remember the Orchard, don't you?"

My gaze swept across the long rows of trees spreading out as far as the eye could see. The outside wall of the UnSeelie Court surrounded the Orchard though I'd never gone so far to find the end of it. Near the front part of the Orchard there was a door that led back into the human realm. One of the only exits out of the Fae world. Unlike the other doors, this one required a key that was specially given out by the queen.

I had one in my pocket but I didn't need it yet. I hadn't found what I came for.

"Why are we here?" I asked, finally unable to handle the suspense. Mab and her son were both drawn to the dramatics. Though, Dorian had tempered since the curse was lifted, or so I'd been told.

"Why to help you, my dear Alice." Mab took me by the arm and drew me further into the Orchard. I thought she was going to take me to where it all started. To the place I'd destroyed so many lives with one simple act but she didn't. She took a left instead of a right and moved along the far side where the bushes covered half the dirt and stone wall.

My eyes widened.

The entrance to the Tree of Life had been closed off before. The bushes growing over the entrance so no one could enter by accident. Now, the bushes had been cleared and the wall had been busted out to an opening seated in the side of the wall.

"I figured that with the Tree gone, there was no harm in opening up the area," Mab mused without me asking a question. "I had someone go in and clear out some of the dead and rotten fruit. The stench had gotten so bad that a strong wind would blow it right into the palace."

I frowned as we stepped into the opening. We walked down a long path at least a dozen meters or more. When we finally reached the end of the path and the sight before me was much different than the last time I had been here.

A large glorious tree taller than I could ever possibly see filled the majority of the hidden alcove. Glowing orange fruit hung from the branches tempting all that dared to venture so far into taking one. I still remembered the taste of it in my mouth. An explosion of flavors rippled through my form, morphing, and changing me until human

Alice was no more and what I was now appeared in her place.

"Tragic, isn't it?"

My head jerked away from the remains of the Tree of Life, a dry dead husk of a tree. "What is?"

"All this space and yet no one has thought to make it into a party room." Mab peered around the bare ground where the roots of the tree still poked through.

The last time I'd been here the ground had been lush with grass and fruit that had gotten so ripe it littered the ground. It was a bit sad to see the mighty tree so broken and lonesome.

"What's this?" Mab slithered across the ground, the bottom of her dress never once getting smudged with dirt or grime.

I followed after her until she stopped before a high root. She leaned over the root and pointed. Following her lead, I glanced over the root as well. My head cocked to the side as I tried to make out what it was she was trying to show me.

Then I saw it.

It was small but there, just poking out of the surface. With a thin brown root barely holding the three green leaves up, the tiny sprout had fought against all the odds to push through the surface of the ash and death of the Tree of Life.

"It seems there is hope after all," Mab murmured, giving me a side-eye with a mysterious smile.

I frowned. "But it's only a sprout. There's no way that little thing could possibly stop the sickness." I shook my head in disbelief. "It's more likely to get eaten up by the sickness before it ever grows big enough to help the Underground."

"And yet," Mab straightened and took my hand with hers, "it preserves."

She held my hand over the sprout and warmth spread into my hand. My magic coaxed by Mab's pulled from my center and out through my fingertips. Mine and Mab's magic mingled together and poured down onto the sprout like water from rain clouds. The sprout reached and stretched for the power, growing slightly bigger until it was less than half a meter high. Still, it was much better than it was.

"Will that be enough?" I gaped at what we had done. "Will it stop the sickness from spreading?"

Mab shook her head. "Only time will tell but we must be prepared for anything. A High King would be best," her starlight eyes slid over to me, "even a High Queen would do."

I snorted. "Where would we find one of those? Kat's not going to do it."

Shrugging an elegant shoulder, Mab stepped away from the sprout. "We never know what we're capable of until we do it. I was never meant to be queen and yet here I am." She glanced over her shoulder at me. "You were never to be Fae and yet you are. Never underestimate one's potential."

Pursing my lips, I chased after her. "I'm only Fae because I cheated. You all know it. I ate from the Tree of Life and made a wish and here I am. I have the magic of a Fae but not the mindset. The way I see it, I'm lucky to have even made it this far and part of that is likely due to the fact that I was locked up for so many years."

"Or you were waiting."

I frowned at Mab. "Waiting for what? Hatter? Because as far as I can tell, he would have been better off without me. He wouldn't have ended up in the Bandersnatch had he not been involved with me when I got caught.

Why haven't you exiled me from the UnSeelie Court all together? I know Kat is the only thing keeping her mother from kicking me to the human realm for good."

Mab paused and turned to me. "You want to know why I have not sent you away? Is that really the question that keeps you up at night? That makes your heartache and your bones tug at you."

"Ugh!" I threw up my hands and stalked in a circle. "You and your damnable riddles. Why can't you say anything like you mean it? Just tell me what I want to know!"

Sighing, her patience with my temper tantrum coming to an end. "So old and yet so much like the child you once were, Alice."

I glared at her still.

"Very well, no more games as you will." Mab stepped up to me and I flinched as she reached out a hand. Her fingers brushed through my blonde curls and she cocked her head to the side. "I do not fault you, Alice. We all wish to be what we are not at some time or another. You were just given the chance to take it."

I stared at her with puzzlement.

"I had such a chance once," Mab continued with a forlorn sigh. "I could have had it all. The High King and all the power that went with it and yet I could not bring myself to do what was necessary to take what I wanted."

My mouth dropped open slightly at the new information. "So, you are...you're the woman..."

Mab's gaze grew sad. "It is hard to forget past mistakes. Even for a queen such as myself." Releasing my face, she composed herself. "Do not pity me, child. For I found love in another more unexpected place. Unfortunately, I have yet to be able to make that love permanent either. But I will, someday."

She paused for a long moment, staring off at nothing.

"So," Mab suddenly turned to me with a wistful smile. "What shall we do about your Hatter? Have you checked his home?"

I groaned. "I tried to but nothing is where it's supposed to be."

Mab nodded in understanding. "Yes, the Underground can be quite a fickle creature. We shall just have to go around her." She winked at me conspiring and looped her arm through mine, dragging me to Reaper only knew where now.

MAB DREW ME BACK to the palace where Mop and Trip were waiting. They sat at a long banquet table covered in a vast array of foods.

When they saw us, Trip jumped up in his seat and waved at me with one claw. The other one had a pastry with raspberry jam in the center. Trip also had raspberry jam around his mouth and stuck to his fur. "Alice! Look pretty Alice, breakfast. Yummy pastries. Yes, yes. So yummy."

I smiled at the opalaught as I came upon the table. "Yes, I can see that." I dropped into a chair next to Mop, hoping he at least wouldn't spray his food all over me when he talked. "How's your food treating you?"

Mab slipped gracefully into a chair at the head of the table, a servant quickly rushed to her side and filled her plate.

Mop swallowed his mouthful and answered, "Good. The palace food be almost as good as me wife's." Mab arched a brow at him and Mop hurried to add on, "Did I say it be almost as good? Better! The best!" He shoved a large piece of bread into his mouth smartly, keeping it from getting even more of his shoe.

Glancing at what was available, I picked a few grapes off a tray and placed them on my plate. Cheese and meats were next before a large glass of orange juice. I had never been much for eating right when I woke up but for some reason today my stomach growled for sustenance. Probably because I hardly ate anything before I went to sleep the night before and hadn't eaten before then either.

At least I didn't actively have to feed off the dreams of humans like some of the Fae. Just being near humans was enough for me to suck off the energy that I needed. While food and air kept me alive, human dreams kept me from aging and my magic up. The Underground would be as sad and normal as the human realm if we weren't able to get the resources we needed.

"So," I began popping a grape into my mouth and chewing it around. I swallowed before continuing as my mother taught me. "There's a sprout of the Tree of Life growing."

"What?" Mop cried out spitting food all over me.

Well, so much for that theory.

I swiped my napkin over my face and neck as Mop settled back down. "Yes, but her majesty and I don't know if it will be enough to stop the sickness."

Mop and Trip drooped in their seats once more.

"But all is not lost my dears," Mab's lips quirked at the edges. "There is still time to find a High King or Queen," Mab's eyes flickered over to me briefly, "before it gets worse."

"Couldna we be gettin' a temporary Fae to sit on the throne?" Mop looked to the queen with a frown.

My eyes lit up. "Yes, that. What he said. Couldn't someone sit on the throne just until the sickness went away and the sprout had time to grow into a full tree?" Hope filled my chest at the prospect. I could probably get Kat to agree to a temporary position but a permanent one? That was as likely to happen as pigs flying.

Mab shook her head and my stomach dropped. "One cannot simply become High King on a whim. They are tied to the Underground for now and forever. The only way to sever that link is for them to die."

Huffing out a breath, I plopped my face into my hand and popped another grape into my mouth. Of course, it wouldn't be that easy. That was the problem with fairy tales. Nothing ended the way you wanted to. The princess doesn't wake up from her deep sleep with a kiss and the slipper never fits and no one lives happily ever after.

"Beg yer pardon, yer majesty but where should we be goin' next?" Mop bowed his head several times which looked silly in his chair.

"You're not going anywhere," Mab replied with a sigh. "You two need to go home to your families where you belong. If you can get them out of the Underground and spread the word. We have to save as many as we can before it gets worse."

I nodded in understanding, shifting toward Mop. "She's right. You need to help everyone get out. We'll send word to Kat so she knows what's going on."

"But Trip and Mop help Alice, Hatter said. Hatter said!" Trip jumped in his chair, his tail smacking the table making it shake.

"Trip be right. We canna leave ye on yer own. Hatter would have me head." Mop reached out and placed his hand on mine.

I snorted. "Hatter doesn't know where his head is half the time. I doubt he would take yours." I patted his hand reassuringly. "I can handle it from here. I promise."

Mop and Trip didn't seem convinced but they didn't argue further through the meal. Once we sent them on their way, I turned to Mab and asked, "What am I going to do next? You said the only way to beat the Underground from moving things on me was to go around. How exactly do I do that?"

Practically melting out of her chair, Mab swept across the room without a word. Assuming I was supposed to follow her, I jumped from the table and hurried after her.

Servants, guards, and members of the court moved out of her way and bowed as we passed by. None of them seemed to quake in fear the way they did with the Seelie Queen, something I always found amusing. The Queen of all the unwanted, misplaced, and monstrous Fae was the most beloved while the White Queen did her best to push anyone away that wasn't her ideal picture of Fae beauty.

Smiling to myself at the thought, I followed Mab as we made our way up a set of stairs and then down a long corridor. She stopped before a dark wood door and turned to me with a serious expression.

"What I am about to share with you, very few have seen. It is a privilege and an honor and I expect you to treat it that way." Mab waited until I nodded my consent before turning the doorknob. Pushing the door open, she revealed a bedroom. Her bedroom.

A four-poster bed sat in the middle of the room covered in a dark comforter and shimmering pillows. A desk stood to one side of the room with neat piles of paper sitting on a tray. A large wardrobe of the same dark oak as the bed sat on the other side of the room. Fae creatures were carved into the wood, faeries, satyrs, nymphs. A door I assumed led to the bathroom was located next to the wardrobe but what pulled my gaze the most was a large curtain covering half of one of the walls.

Mab led me over to the curtain where she reached for the dark vaguely transparent material. "The last one was broken by my son and Katherine. I've had to be more careful with how much I use it with the Shadows still running around over there."

"Do you get to talk to him much?" I couldn't help but ask. It was partly my fault Dorian was stuck in the Shadow Realm, though from what I heard from Kat he wanted it that way.

"Here and there. He's adjusting well enough but misses home. We'll all be happy when this is all over with and the Shadows are gone for good." She sighed and pulled the curtain back to reveal a large mirror. Unlike the mirror back at Kat's, this one was dark and had an inky surface.

Taking a step closer, I inspected the glass. It seemed normal enough and didn't give off any weird vibes like some mirrors I'd seen. "Where am I going with this?"

Mab slid her finger down the edge of the frame the way that Kat did and gestured inside. "You can't go to Hatter's because he does not own a teleportation mirror, so you have to go to the next best thing."

"And that is?" I drew out trying to think of who had another mirror.

"Cheshire's."

My brow lifted. "Oh, I forgot he had one. Probably because I try to stay out of his place." I wrinkled my nose. "I swear that feline had more shoes than Kat and I combined plus it smells as if he and Kat spend all their time..." I trailed off realizing who I was talking to. My cheeks flushed as I ducked my head. "You probably don't want to hear about your almost daughter-in-law with her new lover, do you?"

Mab shrugged. "It doesn't bother me. I'm glad Katherine has found happiness. Just like you, she has always been the daughter I never had. I wish her nothing but the best. Now if only my son could find his own then everything would be complete."

Unsure of what to say to that, I turned my attention back to the mirror. "Should I just..."

"Yes, just like the other mirrors. Think of where you want to go, and you'll end up there. Usually. Try not to let your mind wander." She warned before giving me a slight push in the mirror's direction.

Frowning at her nagging, I closed my eyes and pictured Chess's house. A tall willow tree, the branches hanging down all around it. The deep emerald green grass and purple colored flowers leading up to the base of the tree. The inside of his house a splash of pink and purple on every surface made my nose wrinkle in distaste. Kat and I had tried to get him to change it but he insisted it stay that way.

"Now, Alice. Go," Mab murmured in my ear, her hand on my back.

With her assurance, I stepped forward into the mirror. The cool gelatin liquid surrounded me instantly, pulling and tugging me in the direction I needed to go. I kept the image of Chess's house at the forefront of my mind until finally I was pushed out the other side.

I tripped over the frame of the mirror on my way out and ended up on the pink shag rug staring up at the wooden ceiling. A shadow bent over me and Chess's cheeky grinning face stared down at me.

"Why Alice, I didn't know you were coming over today."

I groaned as he offered me a hand up. "I hadn't expected on coming if I were to be honest but the Underground decided to keep moving. So, each step I got closer to Hatter the further away I got."

Chess cocked his head to the side. "That does sound like our girl." He collapsed on a chair and threw his leather pant clad legs up on a violet stool. "What can I do for you?"

"Well, first off, we need to get a hold of Kat." I reached into my pocket and found my compact mirror. I touched the sides but couldn't get it to come on. Turning to Chess, I asked, "Do you mind?"

Holding his hand out, Chess took the mirror and swiped his finger along the surface, it rippled as it activated. "You're welcome."

"Kat really does need to figure out a mirror that anyone can activate," I complained as Kat's face appeared on the surface.

"But then what would make me special?" Kat answered my comment with a grin.

I scoffed, shifting to sit down on one of the nearby chairs. "Like it would kill you? Your head is already too big as it is."

Kat frowned mockingly. "That's not very nice. And here I thought you were calling to talk, not make fun of me."

"I did," I assured her with a smirk. "The other part is just an added benefit."

Huffing in mock annoyance, Kat asked, "So what's the what?"

I glanced over at Chess and then back to Kat. "You're about to have a whole lot of company very soon."

Kat's brows furrowed. "What?"

"Mab has requested Mop and Trip to spread the word and send all who can to the human realm until we can get the sickness stopped."

Her mouth dropped open. "What? Where the hell does she expect me to put all of them? I don't have the time or the accommodations to handle that large of an immigration on such short notice." She began to breathe heavily and a brown paper bag came out of nowhere.

Chess appeared beside me instantly. "Pet, breathe. Remember what the doctor said. Just breathe."

"Doctor," I glanced up at him and then back at Kat. "What doctor? Kat, what's wrong? Do I need to come back?"

"No, no," Kat said through breathing. "No. I'm fine. Just the doctor said I had to keep my stress level even or it could..." she trailed off and gave Chess a look over my shoulder. He nodded. With a small smile, Kat lowered the paper bag. "It could hurt the baby."

"Baby!" I screamed so loud that they could probably hear me all the way in the Seelie Court.

"How could you not tell me you're pregnant?" I cried into the mirror, my heart pounding so quickly I feared it might fly out of my chest.

Chess chuckled at my reaction as Kat beamed at me.

"We just found out a few days ago," Kat dipped her head, a bit shy for once in her life. "We were going to tell my parents today before all this," she waved her hand vigorously around, "happened. Which, babe," she shifted her eyes to Chess.

I moved the mirror so she could see him completely.

"Yes, pet?"

"Hurry up and get your ass back here, I want some fried pickles." When I made a disgusted sound, she added on, "Don't judge me. Pregnancy cravings."

Chess rolled his eyes. "You're only six weeks in, kitten. The cravings won't start for another month. You're just addicted to fried food."

She stuck her tongue out at him. A clanging sounded in the distance causing Kat to frown. "Hold on a second." Her mirror bobbed as she walked.

Chess and I waited patiently while she opened her door and greeted her guests.

"Mop! Trip! I didn't expect you to get here so soon." Kat's surprise was clear in her voice. The mirror turned, showing me both of them. "Say hi to Alice, everyone!"

Everyone?

Then I noticed that it wasn't just Mop and Trip but their whole family.

"Let me through," A female brownie commanded, pushing past Mop and into Kat's home. "I need ta see what we be workin' with. Ah! Faeries on toast! What a mess ye made of yer home. Donna ye ever dust ye silly girl."

Mop huffed and chased after her. "Love, donna be criticizin' the Moderator. We be guests."

While they argued, Trip and his wife, Petal, were counting the children.

"Nine, ten, wait," Petal frowned and searched the porch. "Where's Tolum? Tolum?"

"Here, mum!" an opalaught smaller than all the others popped his head out from behind the group.

Grinning from ear to ear, Trip turned back to the mirror. "Trip loves his big family, Trip does. But so many children is hard to keep up with. Yes, it is."

I covered my mouth to stifle a giggle, clearing my throat, I said. "I'm glad you all made it over alright. Did you warn the others?"

Trip bobbed his head as his family moved into Kat's house. "Yes, yes. Trip and Mop sent messages through the flowers. Yes Trip and Mop did."

I frowned. "Are you sure everyone will get it that way?"

"Oh, yes. Oh, yes. Everyone listens to the flowers. Yes, they do." Trip primly nodded. "Much more than Mop and Trip. Trip expect them to come any time now." His head swiveled, his ears perking up at a sound I couldn't make out. "Oh, there they are. Yes, there!"

"Oh, fuck." Kat groaned, turning the mirror back to her. "I gotta go. My house is about to be overrun with Fae. I have to go. Call me with any updates." The mirror went dark before I could respond back.

I turned to Chess, my brow furrowed. "Do you think she'll be alright?"

Chess pushed his braided pink hair off his shoulder and shook his head. "Not likely. She's been on edge ever since we found out. The doctor said she has to keep her blood pressure down or she will end up on bed rest."

"Then you should go to her," I insisted, placing a hand on his arm. "I wouldn't forgive myself if anything happened to your baby."

"No. It's alright. Kat will call her mother to help out. She loves the whole publicity of helping the Fae in need." He grimaced at the words but gave me a stubborn frown. "I came to help you find Hatter. So, here I am. It'll be faster if we both are looking for him."

My chest tightened with emotion. "Thank you, so much Chess. Your father would have been so proud of you."

Chess cocked his head to the side. "My father? Oh, yes. I forgot you met him."

It was my turn to be confused. "Did I?" I searched my mind for some remembrance of him but only came up with a pink and purple colored cat. "I don't remember meeting him in any real sense. He only gave me directions once." I pulled my lower lip into my mouth and gnawed on it. Why was this bothering me so much? Cheshire didn't mean anything to me. Cheshire Senior, I mean. But what if he did and I just didn't remember?

I sighed and threw up my hands. "I haven't been remembering things correctly lately, so if I remember any at all, count it as a blessing. Come on, I want to check Hatter's house. If luck is on my side, then he'll be there and this will all be over."

"One can hope." Chess winked at me.

We headed for the door but I paused. My eyes locked onto a nearby chair. That aching in my heart was there again.

I stroked the top of the chair and tried to force whatever memory I had lost to my mind. I couldn't quite forge a picture but voices filled my head.

"Very well. Let's get on with it. Hatter will be here shortly, and I don't want to have to explain this to him." That voice belonged to me. What was I doing here?

"What does that mad old man have to do with anything?" I couldn't place the voice but I knew it somehow. Why?

A sing-song voice responded from another familiar yet unknown origin. *"Oh, didn't we tell you? They're engaged to be engaged. Well, as soon as she tells her human that she's leaving him."*

I'd been here when I was engaged to Lewis *and* Hatter. So something had happened to me between the time I accepted Hatter's proposal and when I ended it with Lewis.

How had I forgotten this?

"Alice?" Chess touched me on the shoulder. "What is it?"

My lips tugged down at the edges. "Uh, I don't know. I think I—" I stared at the chair willing something to come forward...anything. Sighing, I shook my head and smiled at him. "Nothing. I just thought I heard something."

Chess glanced around the room and then shrugged, his tail whipping around in interest. "I don't hear anything. Are you sure you're okay? Perhaps, we should get you back to the human realm. The sickness could have —"

"I'm fine," I cut him off and turned toward the door. "Let's go."

Giving me one more long look, Chess stalked toward the door. Instead of opening it, he walked straight through it. I sighed and walked to the door. Before I stepped through, the first voice came again.

"I won't bite you again. Not unless you beg for it."

I turned back to the room and said, "Never."

HATTERS AND TIGERS, OH MY!

THE HEEL OF MY shoe sank into the emerald green grass. Light peered through some of the long branches of the willow tree giving the area a kind of twilight feel.

Walking around the tree to the front, I frowned at the base of it. "What happened to your chair?"

Chess came up beside me. "I'm in the human realm the majority of the time now. Didn't seem to make sense to leave it here."

"But didn't Kat move it in the first place?" I inquired curiously. "Why move it back at all?"

Smirking, Chess leaned against the base of the tree. "Sometimes it's nice to feel important and my chair has certainly felt like a throne to me."

Frowning at his explanation, I wondered aloud, "And do you feel important now?"

A contented kind of dreamy look covered Chess's face. "I have Kat and now a child coming — something I never expected to ever have. Even if I wasn't the moderator on this side of the portal, that would be enough for me."

I inclined my head.

Before Kat came into his life Chess had been at the mercy of the Seelie Queen. She treated him like an errand boy and her own personal whore, pimping him out to anyone who gained her favor. Then Kat came along and changed all our lives forever.

"We better get a move on." Chess pushed away from the trunk of the tree and made his way down the pathway sprinkled with pink flowers. "I don't want to be caught out there when night falls, do you?"

Following after him, I shivered in displeasure. There were many things in the Underground that preyed on anyone who dared enter their territory at night. I didn't want to be one of those who was caught unaware.

We came to the end of the path and the willow branches parted like a curtain for Chess and me. I moved quickly through the opening and then cried out in pain.

Spinning around, my hand clutching my backside, I glared at the tree branch. "Excuse me!"

The branch swooped around in a gesture I could only define as rude before dropping back down with its mates.

Chess chuckled as I scowled and glared at the tree. "It's not funny. You need to teach that tree some manners."

Chess shrugged lazily. "It keeps the riff-raff out."

I snorted unladylike. "Can't keep the riff-raff out if you're part of the riff-raff."

Spinning on his heel to walk backward, his tail swinging from side to side behind me, Chess smirked. "I never said which riff-raff."

Rolling my eyes. I walked past him and into the woods. Chess caught up with me and for a moment we just walked in companionable silence. After a few moments, I realized this was the first time we had been alone without Kat and I didn't really know what to say.

Thankfully, Chess had no problem filling the empty space. "So, you can't remember much from before the Hall of Mirrors, huh?"

"What?" My head jerked toward him so hard.

Chess trailed his fingers along the trees we passed, his eyes scanning around us. "You mentioned not remembering things and Kitten told me the Hall of Mirrors messed with some of your memories. Including most of what happened with you and Hatter."

I crossed my arms over my chest. "That was confidential."

Chess gave me a lopsided grin. "Not to me. You tell Kat and you might as well tell me. Woman can't keep a secret to save her life."

I giggled. "True. It will definitely be interesting to see how she is pregnant. Ten to one she will blow something up in the first trimester."

Chuckling, Chess nodded. "Too true but you're not going to change the subject."

I sighed and stared down at the ground. "I remember some things. I remember meeting Hatter and a few things from when I was a child, but most things are just feelings."

"What kind of feelings?" He smacked a low hanging branch and then ducked as it tried to swat him back. "Like you left the kettle on?"

I curled my hand to my chest and blinked back the emotions billowing up. "Not exactly. At first, it was just an itch. A kind of prickling on the back of my neck like someone is watching me. Does that make sense?"

Chess nodded. "Maybe someone is? There are plenty of Fae in the Shadow Realm who spend the majority of their time watching those they left behind."

My brows rose. "The Shadow Realm? You mean spirits? That's a bit unsettling."

Shaking his head, Chess explained, "No, the ones the White Queen banished there."

I pursed my lips. "You shouldn't call her that."

Chess shrugged. "Why should I fear her? Kat keeps her mother in check well enough. Besides, she doesn't have much power nowadays anyway with the council making most of the decisions for her now."

"Still," I implored, stepping over a root. "It's not very polite." I waited a moment and then asked, "You've been to the Shadow Realm. Who did you see there?"

"Well, my father for one."

My eyes widened and I stopped in place. "Your father? What is he in there for?"

Chess shook his head and barked a laugh. "Of course, you don't remember. That's just fabulous."

I caught up to him right before the clearing of Mercury's home. "Hold on, Chess. What don't I remember?"

Ignoring my question, Chess gestured to the clearing. "I thought you wanted to find Hatter. Though, I think we're wasting our time here."

My gaze drifted over to the clearing. The long table normally covered in a red tablecloth was bare and the tops of the wood marred with claw and teeth marks. Almost every chair was tipped over and the ground was littered with broken teapots and cups.

We cautiously stepped into the clearing being mindful of the broken glass as we walked.

"What happened here?" I asked more to myself than to Chess.

Chess shook his head, his gaze darting around suspiciously. "I don't know but I don't want to hang around to find out." He swung his arm to the side. "Come on, let's check Hatter's house and get out of here."

Nodding my agreement, I stayed close to Chess as we made our way to Mercury's house.

Unlike the table, Mercury's house was as I remembered it. A crooked roof with crooked walls. The shutters and doors were a bit worse for wear, the paint chipped, and a few shutters were off their hinges. There was no light from the inside, but I tried the door anyway.

It opened easily.

"Doesn't Hatter lock his door?" Chess mused with disbelief. "He has no security system to keep out undesirables.

I scoffed. "Hatter's not here the majority of the time. He probably didn't want to bother with it." I scowled into the darkness. "I can't see a thing in here." Pushing some magic into my hand, I threw the ball of light into the air. The room lightened instantly.

"That's better." I walked around Hatter's home, picking up random books and discarded teacups as I went.

"He's a bit of a slob. Isn't he?" Chess mused, glancing around the dusty room.

I gave him a pointed look. "You're one to talk. I've seen your closest."

Huffing, Chess walked into the bedroom.

Just as I was getting ready to move on a loud roar vibrated the ground beneath us. A teacup sitting on a side table crashed to the floor. I flinched against the sound.

Chess raced into the living area with me, his eyes wide. "What in the world is that?"

I shook my head and my hands covered my ears at the ear-splitting sound. "I have no idea."

Chess stepped toward the door. I grabbed his arm.

"You don't know what's out there."

Giving me a reassuring smile, Chess patted my hand. "So worried about me, Alice? There was a time you only cared about yourself."

I sniffed and released him. "If you die, I'll never hear the end of it from Kat. Plus, I'll have your fatherless child on my conscience and no one should grow up without a father."

Chess gave me a strange look and then said in a somber tone, "But you already have a fatherless child on your head."

I frowned and cocked my head to the side. Unfortunately, I didn't get the chance to ask him about it further because another ear-splitting roar filled the air followed by a scratching at the door.

Chess and I rushed to the window. Standing on either side of the glass, we peaked out between the tattered curtains. A large snout came into view filling up the entire window. We jumped back into place and froze.

The snout huffed and sniffed before backing away from the window. A loud thunk and crack sounded, making me jump and we scrambled back from the window. I thought the creature was trying to break through the door but when nothing burst through, we inched back to the window.

I met Chess's gaze and we peaked back around the corner.

Lounging on top of the now broken table was a large feline of sorts. The creature rampaging around Hatter's home was a ten-foot-tall purple and black tiger. His bright green eyes stared at the house intently, not moving even when those big orbs locked onto us.

I pulled back and looked at Chess. My heart pounding in my chest as I mouthed, a tiger.

Chess frowned in response and then peered back out the window. I chanced a look back out as well.

The tiger Fae didn't even seem interested in us anymore as his long tongue stroked along his paw. A creak sounded and I glared down at my traitorous feet as the tiger's head swiveled back toward us.

"Do you think it's safe to go out?" I asked in a low whisper. "I've never seen such a Fae before."

Chess was still frowning. "I have."

Then without warning, Chess walked away from the window and marched right out the front door.

I scrambled after him but stopped when I reached the open door. Curling my fingers around the edge, I watched as Chess slowly approached the tiger.

At first, he didn't seem interested in Chess. Then his ears perked up and his tail swished from side to side, his big emerald eyes locking onto the approaching Fae.

Chess held out a hand and inched toward him. His voice low and calming as he spoke to the tiger, "It's alright. You're okay. We're not going to hurt you."

The tiger's whiskers twitched but he allowed Chess to move closer to him. I didn't dare call out to warn Chess to be careful in case it caused the tiger to change moods suddenly.

Don't die. Don't fucking die. I hadn't been exaggerating when I said I'd never hear the end of it. Kat would roast me alive and shove me into a pie to serve to the Fae in her house if I let her lover and father of her unborn child die.

Chess finally reached the tiger and held his hand out for him to sniff. The tiger tensed and my breath caught. I was sure Chess was about to get snatched up but then at the last second the tiger inhaled deeply and let out a long purr.

Placing a hand on the tiger's nose, Chess scratched it and murmured, "I knew you'd recognize your own son."

My brows shot up.

Son? That was Chess's father?

The large creature was nothing like the small furball that had given me directions when I was a child. How was the Cheshire Cat so big and why was he going off the bin?

Knowing none of my questions could be answered by staying where I was, I released the front door and stepped out into the clearing.

Immediately, Cheshire hissed, and his hair stood up on end as he glared at me. Chess placed his hand in front of his father and murmured to him once more, too low this time for me to hear.

Cheshire settled back down but didn't stop glaring at me.

"Is it safe to come out?" I swallowed and thanked my lucky stars my voice didn't waver.

Chess waved me forward. "Slow. I don't know what's wrong with him." He sniffed the air. "He smells wrong. Nothing like he was in the Shadow Realm."

Taking one small step at a time, I asked, "How did he even get out of the Shadow Realm?"

Shrugging a shoulder, Chess jerked his head to his father. "You'll have to ask him."

My brow creased as I finally stopped a few feet away from the large tiger. There was something familiar about the animal. Something that tugged at my chest, but I wrote it off as something from when I was a child.

"How are we supposed to do that? Can he speak?"

Snorting, Cheshire seemed to be rolling his eyes at me.

"Can he understand me?" I gaped at him and stepped forward slightly. When he growled at me, I stopped again.

"Of course, he can." Chess sat on the edge of the broken table and patted him on the head.

Cheshire gave him an exasperated look.

"Oops." Chess removed his hand with a grin. Then looked at me. "My father can change his form as he wills. Small. Big. Even into a more humanoid shape like myself." He smirked and flipped his braided hair over his shoulder. "Where do you think I get my good looks?"

"Oh, bother." I huffed. "Then why doesn't he change into a form that can speak to us? And why was he making such a mess of things?" I waved a hand around the broken table and scratches in the house.

Chess didn't have an answer for me right away and Cheshire didn't seem to be in any hurry to answer me either. "I don't know. Maybe it has something to do with how he got here and why his scent is so off."

I stepped forward once more, warning me another growl. "Can I check?"

Chess murmured into his father's ear and then gave me a pointed look. After a moment, Cheshire bobbed his head reluctantly.

"Alright. Come closer, but slowly."

Taking small steps, I eased my way forward. I was about a foot away from him when the scent hit me. I covered my mouth and spun away from him, forcing myself not to gag.

Cheshire huffed at my reaction shifting loudly.

"What is it?" Chess implored.

My hand over my nose, I stepped away until the scent lessened. "You can't smell that?"

Chess cocked his head at me curiously. "Yes, but it's kind of a sour smell, not so dramatic as all that."

I coughed and swiped my nose as I shook my head. "You can't smell that?" Chess shook his head. "He has the sickness."

Cheshire snarled at me as if protesting my statement.

"You can argue all you want. You still have it." I stared pointedly at him. "It doesn't make sense though."

"What?" Chess moved away from his father to my side.

I studied Cheshire closely, trying to figure out this new puzzle. "The sickness made all the other Fae weak and decaying at this point. Cheshire shouldn't be running about like this, let alone making such a mess."

"I'd hardly call this a mess." A low rumbling voice came out of the tiger.

Chess turned back to his father. "Oh, now you have something to say."

Cheshire lifted his nose in the air. "If one does not have anything useful to add to a conversation one ought not to speak at all."

I scowled at the feline. "You could have been a bit more forthcoming instead of scaring the daylights out of us."

He shrugged a single shoulder. "It's not my fault you didn't recognize me." He purred low and curled his head until his whole body shifted and rolled against the table. "And after all our lovely times together."

My frown deepened.

"You might as well save it." Chess scowled at his father. "She doesn't remember you."

This had Cheshire sitting up straight, his eyes narrowing on me. "Not possible. I am not easily forgotten."

"Well, get over it." Chess shifted his weight to one side and popped his hip out. "She has and she did. Now, more important than who remembers who, why are you still in that form?"

I interrupted before Cheshire could answer. "What do you mean I don't remember him? I remember you but not like..." I waved my hand at him. "Like this."

Cheshire's lips curled up.

Could cats smile? If not, this one certainly could.

"So, you do not remember this form, but my other. Well, I cannot blame you. It is quite handsome. Many Fae have admired me for it."

"I don't know. Your cat form was cute and everything but I'm more of a dog person myself." I lifted and dropped a shoulder not understanding what he was talking about. "And furthermore, what do you mean it's not your fault we didn't recognize you? Certainly, you smelled us."

"I didn't know your scent as it is now," Cheshire explained, jerking his head toward me, his tail smacking the ground in irritation.

"He means he doesn't know your Fae smell." Chess clarified for me.

"I figured that." I pursed my lips at Chess and turned my gaze back to Cheshire. "I was human then. I'm not anymore."

"I see that." Cheshire's eyes bore into me, more intimate than a cat who had only given me directions one time.

"So, why'd you attack then?" Chess prodded, poking his father in the face.

Cheshire seemed to duck his head in embarrassment. "I wasn't attacking. I was upset."

"What's wrong? Did something happen?" I stepped forward automatically, wanting to comfort him for some reason but stopped when his scent hit me once more. I took a step back and I could breathe again.

Snarling, Cheshire pushed to his feet and growled, "I can't shift. I'm stuck in this form and it's all that damnable Hatter's fault."

BELLS AND PIPERS

MY FIRST THOUGHT WHEN Cheshire finally answered wasn't where's Hatter which it very well should have been.

Instead, I asked, "How did he get you out?"

Cheshire raised his brows at me incredulously. "Why, he struck a deal of course."

"Of course, he did." I groaned and placed my face into my hand. "What did he trade this time?"

Cheshire went silent. Then very slowly as if not wanting to upset me, he murmured, "Himself."

"What?" I shouted so loudly that the birds in the woods flew out and up into the air. "What do you mean he traded himself?"

Cheshire shifted indignantly. "Exactly, as I said. Hatter traded himself for me to get out."

I sank down onto the side of a nearby overturned chair. "But why?" I blinked rapidly my brain not catching up to everything it was being given. "Why would he trade for you? I didn't even think he knew you very well. He certainly never mentioned it this last year."

Cheshire sat up further. "You've been with him for a year?" He stared at me suspiciously. "When exactly did you get out of the Hall of Mirrors?"

Chess stepped between us. "There's no time for this. I already told you she doesn't remember you. So, you might as well take your hurt feelings and stow them for now. We still have to find Hatter and get him out of the Underground before he gets the sickness unless he's already caught it." He looked pointedly at his father.

Cheshire stretched out and yawned. "Don't look at me. I'm not the important one in this story as it's been made abundantly clear."

I frowned at the hurt in his voice. What had I done? Was I supposed to have come for him? I wanted to ask but Chess was right. We had to find Hatter and get him out of here. Cheshire might be immune in some way to the sicknesses' side effects, but I doubt Hatter would be so lucky.

"He's right." I stood and brushed my dress off. Cheshire glared at me. "I mean, Chess is right. We don't have time for this."

"Never have time for this or that. We live forever and yet have no time for anything. What's the point of it all then, I ask?" Cheshire muttered under his breath as if we couldn't hear.

Ignoring his father, Chess turned to me. "So at least now we know where Hatter is. The only problem now is getting to the Shadow Realm."

I tapped a gloved finger on my lips. "We can't go back to the queen to get in. She's already helped me once. Plus, we'd be backtracking to your house and you know how the Underground feels about backtracking. We'll have to find another way in."

"What is wrong with the world now?" Cheshire clipped, clearly pouting. "Everything is backward and not where they were before. I always knew her to be a fickle place, but this is ridiculous even for her."

"It's the sickness," I explained. "Come on, we'll explain on the way." Cheshire stood and stepped toward me, making me gag once more. I stepped back. "Just keep your distance, will you?"

I stalked off before he could protest, leaving him with his son.

"You weren't saying that when I was between your milky thighs."

My face burned as his words reached my ears, more embarrassed than appalled by his words.

"Father!" Chess scowled and then their footsteps were clearly following behind me. "You can't say stuff like that to her."

I kept moving forward, pretending not to be listening.

"Why not? It's true."

Chess huffed. "But she doesn't know that. She doesn't even know that she's responsible for—"

"Shhh," Cheshire hushed his son and then asked, "Alice? Where exactly are we going?"

For a heartbeat, I thought about not answering so they'd keep talking but there were more important things to worry about now.

I stopped by a tree. "I'm not sure exactly." Turning one way and then the other, I frowned. "There are only two ways into the Shadow Realm that I know of and that's the UnSeelie Queen's mirror and the door." Turning around, I looked at Cheshire. "How did you get out?"

Cheshire rubbed himself against a tree and lazily answered, "I didn't come by either. I was in the Shadow Realm talking to the Tweedles and then I wasn't."

Tweedles? Why did that sound so familiar? I was really getting tired of all this nonsense. I didn't know what was real or not in my mind anymore. Then a thought hit me.

"Then how do you know Hatter was the one who saved you and that he took your place?" Chess pointed out before I could.

"Because the mad idiot was standing there when I appeared in the Seelie Queen's castle." He said it as if it were the most obvious thing in the world.

"So, we don't need to go to the Shadow Realm, we need to go to the Seelie Court," I mused aloud.

Cheshire snorted. "And you're just going to leave the Tweedles to their fate? You have changed, Ally."

My mouth twisted to the side. "Why did you call me that? No one calls me that. And what do I care for the Tweedles? I don't know them. Besides, I can barely save the people I do know let alone everyone." I took a deep breath and huffed. "And why is it suddenly my duty to save everyone anyway? I'm just a representative. I'm not the moderator. Ask your son to do it!" I jerked a hand in Chess's direction. "Or better yet someone who actually gives a flying flip about any of it at all."

I turned on my heel and marched away.

"She really has changed," Cheshire's voice followed after me.

"Try being locked up for almost two hundred years all by yourself and see how well you turn out," was Chess's response.

My eyes burned at his words, but I didn't turn back. I didn't apologize. A part of me felt bad for anyone banished to the Shadow Realm. It did. But that wasn't my problem. I was here for one reason and one reason only. To save Hatter. Everyone else would just have to wait for their turn.

"Are you sure you can't change back?" Chess asked his father once more. "If we're going to the Seelie Court, we will attract less attention if you weren't so..." he trailed off and waved his hand at his father's large form. "Big."

Cheshire scowled. "Don't you think I would have done so already if I could? Do you think I like traipsing through the forest at this size? All the branches keep scratching me and the rocks hurt my paws. I'd much rather be in my other form at this moment, even if not to make dear Alice remember me." He gave me a long leering stare that made my insides flip.

Alice, he's a cat. A cat! Why are you getting so worked up over him? Besides, you're with Mercury. You cannot have them both.

A small teasing voice answered in my head, *Why not?*

Pushing the thoughts away completely, I sighed. "Fine. I will try and see if I can get a glamour to work on him, but I wouldn't hold my breath." Remembering his stench, I grimaced. "Actually, I might have to."

Chess held his hand up. "It's alright. I'll try my hand at it."

Cheshire sat down on his hind legs and huffed. "I don't see what all the bother is, any Fae worth their magic is going to see straight through my glamour."

Smirking at his father, Chess cracked his fingers. "Not this one. My kitten and I have a heart bond, so our magic is shared."

"You still have a heart bond with the Seelie Queen's daughter?" Cheshire's eyes widened. "And she hasn't killed you off yet."

"As I've told you before, Kat is nothing like her mother and for your information we're doing quite well and are in fact expecting." He smirked and surveyed his father. "Now hold still, you haven't had a glamour done until you've had it done by a moderator."

"Expecting?" Cheshire cried out and jumped up. "How do you expect me to sit still after that kind of news? I'm going to be a grandfather!" He smiled brightly at Chess and then stepped toward me as if he were going to hug me, but I stepped back. Frowning at my reaction, Cheshire turned back to his son. "Why didn't you tell me before? Is she very far along? Does the queen know?"

Chess sighed. "I shouldn't have told you. Now you'll never settle down."

I leaned on a nearby tree and chuckled, "You might as well tell him, or he'll pester you for hours. He's quite insatiable."

Cheshire's head swiveled around to look at me. "You do remember me! You cheeky little thing."

My mouth dropped open as I bolted up, my hands in front of me. "I don't know what you're talking about. I don't even know where that came from. I promise. If I knew you, I would say so. I cannot lie, remember?"

All the excitement in Cheshire faded away. He sank back down on the ground, his shoulders bunched and his tail drooping. Once more I had this urgent need to comfort him. I squashed it down firmly, wrapping my arms around my waist.

"Can we get on with this already?" I snapped at Chess before turning my back on both of them.

Chess made an annoyed sound and then was silent. After a moment, he muttered, "Damn. I so thought that would work."

I twisted slightly to look over my shoulder. Cheshire was still a tiger but now his fur was more pink than purple.

"Perhaps, I could force you to shift?" Chess offered hopefully. "I wouldn't be forcing your body to hide what you are, just changing you into one of your normal forms? What do you think?"

"Fine. Whatever. Just get on with it." Cheshire breathed out heavily, not at all interested in being changed or whatever anymore.

"You know you could be a bit more helpful." Chess held his hands up and focused once more. "Do you even know how you got stuck in this form?"

"No."

I had a thought. "Were you in this form when you were transported out of the Shadow Realm?"

Cheshire glanced over my way. "Yes. Not that it matters."

"It might," I added on quickly. To Chess, I said, "He might be stuck because of the teleportation magic used to shift him from one realm to the other. They are quite tricky and if performed incorrectly can lead to dismemberment, death, or even —"

"Do you have a point to all of this?" Cheshire snapped at me.

I narrowed my gaze at him. "Temporary magic paralysis."

Chess frowned. "So, you're saying it's only temporary? How long will it last?"

I shrugged. "It depends on the caster and the distance. How long have you been out of the Shadow Realm?"

Cheshire glanced up at the sky a bit more interested in what I had to say. "A few sun cycles at least." His head dropped back down as he stared at me curiously. "How do you know so much about teleportation magic?"

Feeling self-conscious, I tugged on my kid gloves and flicked the color from white to pink to purple. "I had a lot of time on my hands and an endless supply of books to read." I left it at that, finally shifting my gloves back to white and then turned on my heel. "It'll wear off on its own any minute now. With any luck it'll be gone before we even reach the Seelie Court."

A SIGHT WORTH SEEING

TO MY UTTER SURPRISE, the Underground actually stayed in one place, allowing us to get back to the initial stone labyrinth quite easily.

Unfortunately, without a short cut like Mop had through Teeth, we had to go the long way around.

"You know, they really should make it easier to get around here," I said over my shoulder to the two felines following a few feet behind me. "The humans have cars, planes, trains, even boats that can zip you to wherever you want to go. We have magic.

There has to be something we can do similar to that."

Chess snorted. "Why don't you bring it up at the next High Council meeting...oh wait...you can't because we don't have one."

I pursed my lips and huffed. "I don't know why everyone insists I can find the next High King or Queen. My mother hardly gave me any responsibilities when I was human. I only had to sit pretty, keep my mouth shut and hope a rich gentleman would marry me." I paused and smirked. "I guess that didn't really turn out too well now did it?"

Chess chuckled behind me, while his father asked, "What's so funny?"

"Don't you get the gossip in the Shadow Realm?" Chess asked him.

"Only some of it. Most of those banished don't have much to share."

"Well, you're Alice isn't quite as innocent as she once was—"

"Chess," I said, casting a warning loop over my shoulder.

Smirking at my reaction, he stopped and told his father in a conspiring tone. "You know how dear Alice was engaged?"

I paused as well. While I didn't need any more people knowing my dirty laundry, I was curious to see how Cheshire would react. He seemed to know me. Did he know this?

Cheshire peered at me in a peculiar way for a tiger, his head tipped to the side and his ears twitching. "Yes," he drew out slowly. "What of it?"

Sliding his tongue along the sharp edges of his canines, Chess crossed his arms over his chest and leaned against a nearby wall. "Do you know how she got unengaged to him?"

Cheshire cocked his head slightly. "No. The Seelie Queen's guards had already gotten a hold of me before I even knew why I was being arrested."

I frowned. "Arrested? Why were you arrested?"

"Off-topic," Chess waved me off and straightened. "Well, while you were off in dreamland dear innocent Alice, who wouldn't hurt a fly—"

I gritted my teeth and bit out, "You go too far, cat."

"I'm almost there." Chess assured me as I took a step toward him. "Anyway, she snuck back to the human realm and —"

A pipe playing interrupted Chess, pulling all of our attention back toward the path.

"What is that?" I angled my head to hear it better.

It was like chiming bells—a lovely melody I wanted to dance to and play. A euphoric feeling came over me as my feet moved on their own accord.

Chess and Chesire followed after me caught in the tune themselves.

We zigged and zagged, following the sound until we turned a corner and walked into a small cleared out area. In the center was a fountain of scantily dressed women pouring water out of their nipples and buckets. Each corner of the area had a tall green-leafed tree. The music came from one of the trees.

I stepped toward the music, my feet skipping and twirling to the sounds. A small shadow hid behind the tree and shifted closer to the corner as I approached.

"Don't hide," I cooed to the creature, not aware of the danger we were in. "We just want to dance to your lovely music."

The shadow crept closer, its big brown eyes peering out around the trunk of the tree with a pipe up to its mouth. When it completely stepped out, it was quite a bit older than I thought with a humanoid top half and a goat lower half. Short horns protruded through the head where his hairline was seriously receding.

Had I been in my right mind, I'd have found him repulsive, but the music combed over any of my anxieties, making everything warm and wonderful.

"What shall we do?" Chess purred, coming up beside me, his arms wrapping around my waist and his tail sliding up my leg. He'd never been this familiar with me, but I didn't seem to care.

The creature switched the tune and I had the sudden urge to ride the Cheshire like a horse.

Spinning away from Chess with a giggle, I danced toward the tiger.

However, not even the pipe's music could overcome the stench of sickness coming off of Cheshire. The moment it hit my nose, my mind cleared, and I froze.

My head jerked from side to side as I tried to figure out how I'd even gotten there. Cheshire rubbed against my leg, his snout pushing under my skirt.

I shoved him away with a scowl. "Snap out of it, you idiot." When Cheshire kept insisting on licking my thigh, I reached out and pinched his ear between my fingers, giving it a twist.

A low roar filled the clearing.

"What was that for?" Cheshire snarled at me and then blinked. "How did we get here?"

"My thoughts exactly." I turned away from him. "Now for Chess." I froze at what I saw, my face going beat red.

"What is my son doing with that satyr's horns?" Cheshire angled his head to the side, his brows drowning down. "Should we stop him?"

"We should stop him," I quickly answered and stepped away from him. Thankfully, the pipe didn't affect me this time as I stalked toward Chess and the satyr.

The Satyr paid no mind to me, his eyes rolling back into his head. I grabbed Chess's tail and gave it a good yank.

"What the mother fucking pixie fuck!" Chess glared at me but then looked down in the position he was in wrapped around the Satyr and quickly backed away. "Piper! When did you get another pipe?"

The satyr groaned and lowered the wooden instrument. "Oh, come on I was almost there."

I made a gagging sound.

Chess reached out and tried to grab the pipe, but Piper was too quick, hopping away quickly. "Come now, you know you're not allowed any instruments after last time. Give it up."

Piper pushed his lower lip out in a pout that only made him all the more disturbing. "But with Romp out with the sickness I have no one to help feed me. I had no choice."

I shook my head and crossed my arms over my chest. I remembered him now. "Feed you? More like raping. You aren't worthy of living, let alone have a pipe. You should count your lucky stars the Moderator didn't knock you down right then and there. In fact," I cranked my fingers and pushed power into my hands, "I elect we take care of you right now."

Piper cowered away from me, clinging to his piper as I reached out to grab him.

"My son was right...you have changed."

Cheshire's words made me pause.

"What would you know of it?" I scowled at him. "You claim to know me, but I have never been anyone but who I am. A little alone time did not change the basis for who I am."

Cheshire hummed, thinking. "The Alice I knew would have been appalled to lift a hand against anyone, even someone deserving of it such as the satyr."

Tired of this game we were playing, I grabbed Piper by the throat and lifted him in the air staring hard at Cheshire the whole time. "The precious Alice you think you know doesn't exist anymore. That Alice was destroyed when she used her new Fae powers against her fiancée to drive him mad for daring to betray her." I squeezed the satyrs throat until he dropped his pipe and began clawing at his neck.

Chess snatched up the pipe with a frown.

Dropping my hand and turning to Cheshire, the satyr crashing to the ground as I said, "You. Do. Not. Know. Me."

I didn't wait for him to respond as I stalked away. I kept moving away from the clearing and toward the setting sun. The way into the Underground laid where the sky ended, and the Labyrinth began. I didn't know how I was going to get out through there, but I had to try. We couldn't very well go back to the castle. There wasn't time.

Not checking to see if the others were following me, my footsteps stomped along the stone ground with more force than I meant.

A small Fae creature, similar to a mouse, popped his head out of the wall. "Hey, watch it. Some of us are sleeping."

Stopping in my tracks, I almost apologized then caught myself. "I will step more lightly. Have a good night."

The creature scowled at me and ducked back into his hole.

Sighing, I leaned against the wall and sank down into a squat. My fingers dug into my hair and I tried to figure out what the heck I was doing.

I should be at home with Mercury. How did I get dragged into all this madness again? This is all the Seelie Queen's fault. If she hadn't put Mercury in the Bandersnatch—

Her fault? Don't you mean, your fault?

No, it's not.

You're the one who had to be Fae.

I know but—

You're the one who made a deal with the Shadow Man to break up the royal couple to get what you wanted.

That's true but still if the Seelie Queen hadn't—

"Are you alright?" A hand touched my arm.

I glanced up from where I had been glaring at the floor. "Uh, yes. Fine. Really. I'm just thinking too much." I scrambled to my feet and sniffed. "Let's go. I want to get this over with and go home."

Chess gave me a disbelieving frown but didn't push the issue.

To my great blessing, both felines were silent on the final leg of the trip. It wasn't until we reached the alcove with the small pond and tree that we had to talk to one another.

"So..." I drew out, staring up at the hole in the tree, "have you ever gone out this way? Is it even possible?"

Cheshire snorted. "Of course, it's possible. This is the Underground."

I pushed my lips to one side, shooting him an incredulous look. "I was quite aware. That does not answer the most important question of how?"

Cheshire opened his jaws to no doubt give me another annoying answer, but a sort of surprised gurgle came from his throat. His body twitched and glimmered for a moment. Then he placed his four legs out in front of him and his head fell forward as he stretched long and lean.

His tail thickened and the hair on his head lengthened. The fur on his body smoothed until all that was left were a handful of stripes along his hips and breast bones.

I swallowed thickly.

The last thing to change was his snout. It shortened and paled, revealing a strong nose and voluptuous lips, leaving his emerald green eyes in place.

Cheshire stood up straight, his pale purple hair falling around him like a curtain shielding parts of his body from my view. Tipped ears peeked out between his hair as he pushed it from his face and turned to us, giving me a full view of the hard planes of his arms and the impressive length hanging between his legs. To say he was more than a little happy to see me was an understatement.

A startled eep fell from my lips.

Lips curling up into a seductive smirk, Cheshire purred, "Well, that's much better."

"FATHER," CHESS COUGHED AND averted his eyes. "Clothing, please."

Cheshire looked down at himself and a sly grin slid up his gorgeous face. "What? I am in my natural state. What is so wrong with that?" His gaze shifted over to me, his tongue peeking out to lick along his fangs. "Besides, it looks like dear Alice enjoys me this way."

I made a choking sound and jerked my head away from him so fast I winced. "Clothing, clothing would be good." I wrapped my arms around my waist and tapped my foot, my shoulders bunched up around my ears as I pretended not to be affected by his nakedness.

With a reluctant sigh, Cheshire said, "Very well. If I must."

"You must," I clipped, turning my head toward him briefly before remembering myself and closing my eyes tightly. "This isn't the time or place for games."

"Oh, Alice dear," Cheshire purred. "You are so wrong. This is exactly the time. The Underground is dying, what else is there to live for if not now?"

"Father," Chess sighed exasperatedly. "You can try and get into Alice's pants or rather skirts later. We have places to be. So, if you please?"

Huffing, Cheshire snapped his fingers. "Fine. There. You may open your eyes now. I am decent."

Not quite believing him, I peeked through my eyelashes before finally opening them completely. Cheshire without clothing was a treat but Cheshire with clothing on was just as deadly.

Loose billowy pants covered his legs and a robe-like material covered his top half though he might as well not be wearing a top at all. He wore the robe mostly opened, barely belted at the waist to keep it partially together. His long purple tail lay over his shoulder like a feathered boa much thicker and longer than Chess's cat-like tail. Cheshire kept his hair long and flowing down around him.

Cheshire's large green orbs turned to me expectantly.

Swallowing down the need to drool over him just a little bit the way Kat did a double chocolate Frappuccino, I jerked my head tightly up and down. "Fine. Let's turn back to the matter at hand. How to get through to the Seelie Court."

"Oh, yes. I can help you there." Cheshire grinned, approaching the tree.

I huffed. "Why didn't you say so in the first place?"

Giving me a sideways look, Cheshire gruffly responded, "I was a bit busy, you know. I didn't have the chance. Though, I'm not complaining about being back in this form. At least, I have hands." He held both hands up and perused all his clawed fingers with great interest.

"Father," Chess prodded his tail, twitching irritably. "The portal."

"Oh, yes." He walked over to the tree, making sure to avoid the pond at its base. His tall height made it quite easy for him to reach up and grab the edge of the hole. His hand glowed a faint purple as he tugged on the edge. "Just have to readjust the threads a bit..." His mouth twisted to the side in concentration.

It was such an intriguing sight, I found myself moving toward him without knowing it. It wasn't until Chess shouted that I realized I was in danger.

"Alice! Watch out."

Something sharp sank into my ankle. Crying out, I glared down at the featureless white head, its sharp jaws wrapped around my ankle. So entranced by Cheshire, I hadn't paid any attention to where I was stepping, ending up with one foot in the pond and one out. Apparently, pretty men made me as sharp as a feather.

"Get off," I shook my leg and tried to dislodge the disturbing creature. A waft of sickness filled my nose and I covered my mouth trying to hold back the urge to gag and simultaneously shake the creature off.

Two pale hands with purple stripes wrapped around the wrists grabbed hold of the head, pulling at the jaws until they released me. I lost my balance and fell into Cheshire. One arm wrapped around me, while his other threw the featureless head back into the pond.

This close to Cheshire, I expected to be gagging on the sickness smell, but I wasn't. Cautiously, I lowered my hand and buried my face into his chest.

"Not that I do not mind your delicious form pressed into mine," Cheshire purred, both arms holding me now, "but what exactly are you doing?"

"You don't stink," I stated matter of fact.

Cheshire snorted. "Well, I'd hope not. I bathe quite often."

I lifted my head from his chest and frowned at him incredulously. "It has nothing to do with how often you bathe." I pushed away from him and stepped back until the scent of the sickness hit me once more. Groaning and covering my mouth, I took one step forward, leaving only a few inches between us. The scent was gone again. "Curiouser and curiouser."

"What?" Chess stepped up next to me, his head cocked in interest.

"It seems that the sickness is only in the space around your father." I stepped back and instantly plugged my nose, moving my hand over the area in which the sickness laid. "When I'm outside of his aura, I suppose that's a good enough word for it, the sickness tries to keep me away." I frowned and stepped back into Cheshire's personal space. "But once I get past it then... there's nothing. Like the sickness doesn't even exist. How can that be?" I peered up at Cheshire with wide eyes.

Cheshire's lips curled up at the edges. "I do not know, sweet Alice but anything that allows me to have you in my arms once again is alright by me." His hands slid around my waist and he shifted closer to me.

I blushed furiously and disentangled myself from his arms. "Uh, yeah. Anyway," I searched for something to change the subject and my eyes fell on the elongated hole in the tree, "you fixed it!"

"Well, of course, I did." Cheshire whipped around, easily distracted. "It was simple as stretching the particles out and redirecting them to go in as well as out."

"How did you know to do that?" I cocked my head to the side, keeping close to Cheshire but away from his grabby hands.

Smiling broadly, Cheshire purred, "Who do you think made the entrance to the Willow tree in the first place? Displacing particles is what I do."

I nodded pleasantly. "That explains your ability to shift as well. It's fascinating how much magic relies on simple science." Cheshire and I shared a mutual smile of agreement.

Chess came up behind us. "I don't know much about science, but I do know I want to get out of here."

Reluctantly, pulling my eyes away from Cheshire's enchanting ones, I glanced at Chess. "Oh, yes. We should probably go."

Staring into the dark hole, a part of me was apprehensive about going through. I didn't know if it would throw me back out or even rip me apart.

A hand slid around my hip and a warm breath whispered into my ear, "Are you frightened, little one?"

Swallowing thickly, I turned my head slightly to peer into Cheshire's eyes. "Wouldn't you be?"

Cheshire licked his lower lip wetting it. "All good things worth doing should strike a pang of fear in your heart or it's not worth doing."

Entranced by his words, I leaned into his embrace. "Is that so?"

"I wouldn't lie to you, pet." Cheshire dipped his head down, our mouths barely a breath apart.

A throat cleared.

I blinked and jerked away from Cheshire, my face heating. "Uh, yes. We're not going to find Hatter hanging around here."

Without another moment's pause, I stepped out of Cheshire's embrace and through the hole. Instantaneously I was sucked up and spit out the other side. The expression on the guards' faces were enough to make it all worth it.

Every single one of them gaped at me as I walked through the door and into the Between.

Cedric chuckled and shook his head. "Why am I not surprised?"

"What?" I pursed my lips.

"Only you could figure a way into the Between from a door that only goes out."

"Who the mother fuckin'—" A snarling growl came from beside me. The Redhat rubbed his face with his hand, the door having hit him in it when I came through. His eyes landed on me and he paled. "Oh, Representative. No worries. I shouldn't have been standin' so close to the door."

The door swung up once more, smacking the Redhat in the face once more. I winced as the other guards oh'd as Cheshire and then Chess came through the door as well. Everyone but the nymph covered their nose and mouth as the sickness filled the room.

"Why Cheshire, as I live and breathe." The nymph stepped up to the older Fae as unfazed as Chess by his scent. "I thought you were banished?"

Cheshire grinned at the nymph. "Gert, you know nothing can keep me locked up for long."

Laughing joyfully, Gert clapped his hands on Cheshire's forearm and they shook like old friends. "Of course not. You're too sly for that. What are you doing back here? Don't you know there's a sickness going around."

"Uh," I shifted close to Cheshire so I could breathe freely. "Can't you smell it?"

"What?" Gert blinked at me.

"I have the sickness, friend." Cheshire sighed and dragged his claws through his hair.

"Oh," Gert cocked his head to the side. "I didn't realize. You don't look like it."

"You mean, you can't smell it?" I asked, glancing once more at the other guards keeping their distance. Even the receptionist was hiding behind her hand.

Gert shrugged. "Nymphs don't have much of a sense of smell. I couldn't tell a dandelion from a dragon snap."

"Don't feel bad," I explained with a small smile. "Chess can't smell it either."

"I still do not understand why I cannot scent the sickness as you do," Chess huffed, his hands tucked into his armpits.

I glanced over at my shoulder at him. "You're the only one who can't smell it. Mop and Trip smelled it fine enough before. Perhaps, because you are half and half?" I offered up helpfully.

Cheshire growled at me. "His lineage has nothing to do with his Fae abilities. If anything, he has more Fae in him than the average creature. Including you."

I frowned. "No offense meant. I was simply stating what could be the cause of it. It could be his lineage and it could be the fact that he's tied to Kat, who isn't completely Fae herself. She doesn't even have much of an iron allergy."

Placing a hand on his father's shoulder, Chess reassured him, "Alice wasn't being hateful, father. She might be Fae now, but she still has the tact of a human. Not to mention, she hangs around my kitten all the time." He chuckled. "Reaper knows she's not a good influence on anyone."

A handful of guards chuckled as I giggled and covered my mouth with my hand. "True."

Surveying us in a queer manner, Cheshire nodded, "Very well. Those are logical reasons enough and your Kat seems far more interesting the more I hear of her. The brief interaction I had with her did not give me much of an impression of her but if you say so then I will choose to believe you."

"Where are you headed?" Gert asked as the Redhat groaned. "Quickly before the lug head gets his senses back. We don't need to listen to him bitch for the rest of the afternoon."

"To see the Seelie Queen," Cheshire answered.

Frowning, Gert ushered us to the other door. "Have you not found Hatter yet?"

I sighed and shook my head. "Unfortunately, not. We are hoping the queen will have an idea."

One of the guards at the Seelie Court door snorted. "Be prepared to bargain. The queen doesn't give anything away for free."

"This isn't my first rodeo." I got a mixture of confused expressions, except Chess, who grinned. "The human slang is lost on them, isn't it?"

"Very much so." Chess licked his lips and stared off into the distance. "Kat will be pleased to know she has rubbed off on you so much."

I rolled my eyes. "Let's not tell her, alright?"

Fingers crossed, Chess smirked, "No promises."

"Well, are you going or not?" The grumpy guard from before opened the door for us and gestured inside. "We haven't got all day."

"Yes, you do," I retorted primly. "You've got eternity, but you probably should go to the human realm for the time being."

The guard looked at me, incredulously. "And abandon our posts? Never. No sickness will take me down." He huffed and puffed out his chest in his gold armor.

Sighing in defeat, I turned to the others. "Shall we."

C H A P T E R

THE GOLDEN PEOPLE

I HADN'T BEEN TO Summerville in a long time. I actually couldn't remember the last time I'd been in the Seelie Court. It certainly hadn't changed much since then either way.

The cobblestone roads led you through the town and at the end sat the Seelie Queen's castle. It loomed in the distance, a palace of crystal and gold. The Seelie Queen, Tatiana, tried to hide the coldness of her powers behind the lush gardens surrounding the palace but everyone knew it was her daughter, Kat, who had the green thumb.

Tatiana destroyed everything she touched.

Including my Hatter.

"Are we going to stare at the castle all day or get moving?" Chess teased me as he walked a few paces down the empty roads.

Not answering, I followed closely behind him but not too far away from Cheshire. I didn't want to accidentally walk back into the aura of the sickness.

We walked past several Seelie, each of them primped and puffed to perfection. Every one of them in humanoid shape with pointed ears. If they hid their ears, they could have easily been mistaken as humans but the vast array of colors their skin and hair came in would always give them away.

A pale green-skinned woman with bright green eyes moved past us. She gagged and coughed, covering her mouth with a handkerchief. "Oh, Reaper. What is that awful smell?" She sneered as she hurried away quickly.

Several more Fae came in close contact and cried out similarly. From then on, everyone avoided us with their multicolored eyes watching in a mixture of horror and suspicion.

Cheshire scowled, and tucked his hands into the large sleeves of his robe. "I haven't been this unpopular since the queen requested me for her project."

"Project?" My head turned to him. "What project?"

Glancing down at the ground, not looking me in the eyes, Cheshire muttered, "The one that produced my son."

Still a bit confused by his words, I rolled them around in my head. What project? What did it have to do with Chess? Then I remembered.

"Oh, you mean, when the Seelie Queen made a bunch of Seelie and UnSeelie mates to try and make a half baby?"

Cheshire's brows shot up as he finally looked at me. "I didn't think you'd react so nonchalantly about it."

"Why should I care?" I frowned, not understanding the hurt in his voice. "And besides, weren't you in the Shadow Realm? Or was it before? How did you even participate in her attempts to break the spell on her daughter?" I laughed to myself. "Did she pull you out to give an unsuspecting Fae woman a good tumble in the bushes before sending you back again?"

Silence was my answer.

"Oh." I pressed my lips firmly together, my heart aching for some reason. "I wasn't aware. I—"

"I had planned on telling her to stuff it but when you never came for me, I figured I might as well try and find my own way out," Cheshire answered matter of fact.

"When I didn't come for you?"

"It's in the past. Besides," Cheshire wasn't looking at me again, his gaze firmly on the shops and houses we passed by, "as you said before, you don't know me, and I don't know you. It doesn't matter."

Grabbing his arm gently, I stopped him. "It matters to you."

"I was simply comparing the situations," Cheshire began and then drifted off as his eyes caught something over my head.

"What is it?" I twisted around to see what he was staring at.

A shop stood across the road. The windows were dark and the sign above it hung off one of its hinges. The words on the sign faded beyond understanding.

My brows drew together, and I stepped off the sidewalk and crossed the street, not bothering to get out of the way of the oncoming Fae. I had a feeling. What was it? Why did I feel like I'd been to this place before?

Peering into the dusty windows, I could see overturn mannequins and material thrown about as if someone left in a hurry. Scissors and pins lay scattered on the ground and a few half-completed garments hung on dress stands.

I had been here before. I knew it. I just couldn't quite grasp the thought. My fingers touched the boning of my corset, a firm frown on my face and something was triggered.

"I'm a lady. You shouldn't say such words in front of me."

"Which words? There were plenty of words just said. You have to be more specific."

"Is it the word fucking itself or the act of fucking?" He tipped my chin up, his eyes darkening as he spoke. "Because anyone who doesn't like fucking hasn't ever been fucked by us."

A heat spread in between my thighs as I brushed my fingers along my chin. I could still feel his hand there but who was it?

"Who does this shop belong to?" I asked Cheshire and Chess when they appeared behind me.

They didn't answer me at first. Then Chess stepped forward and swiped his hand over the nameplate on the door. "This shop belonged to the Tweedles. They were tailors."

"Were?" I looked away from the inside of the shop, my stomach rolling with the information. "What happened to them?"

Shrugging a shoulder, Chess commented all too carefully, not giving more away than needed, "They were casualties of bad decisions. Come on, the queen will have likely been notified of our arrival already. We best not keep her waiting."

Chess walked away but I stayed where I was, glancing back into the shop, my fingers playing along the laces of my corset.

"They would be so put out to see you so sad, Ally," Cheshire murmured into my ear, his hand taking mine. "Don't let it bother you. They're not dead. Just not here."

Frowning at his explanation, I allowed Cheshire to lead me away from the shop and down the road.

My mind wandered.

There were so many things I didn't remember. Why were they all coming back to me now? They'd had a year to make themselves known, so why now?

My gaze drifted to Cheshire, who looked straight ahead. I hadn't removed his arm from around my waist and found myself snuggling closer to him instead. Why did I feel so comfortable with him? Cheshire claims we know each other a lot more intimately than just a feline giving directions to a lost human girl. And yet...the only memory that connects us is the one back in the Willow Tree.

Then there was the Tweedles. I knew the name. I knew I'd met them before. The voice I'd heard in my head just now was the same one that I'd heard along with Cheshire's. How did I know them? Was I intimate with them as well?

The very thought made my face heat and my skin prickle but not in an unpleasant way.

"A brambleberry for your thoughts?" Cheshire murmured and I glanced up into his hooded emerald eyes.

"Just thinking."

"About?" His claws scratched along the boning of my corset.

"Why can't I remember you?" I said softly, my eyes down on the ground. "Why do I only remember Hatter and even that is kind of murky at the best of times." I glanced back up to Cheshire, my eyes brimming with tears I refused to let fall. "It's like I'm that little girl all over again, thrown into a world I don't know, with rules I can't begin to understand, and I can't trust anything in my head." I grabbed the side of my head and scowled. "I was supposed to have this all figured out already."

Cheshire stopped me, his hand going to the back of my neck.

I stiffened but didn't push him away, interested in what he might say next.

His claw teased my skin behind my ear, making my breath come in shorter pants. "Do not think so hard, Alice. Everything happens for a reason. Perhaps, you had to lose us to really truly have us." He released me with that.

Pursing my lips, I narrowed my eyes at him. "Really? That was it? That's your big reassurance? Everything happens for a reason?" I snorted and crossed my arms over my chest. "I could have gotten that from a fortune cookie."

"There are cookies that see the future?"

Cheshire's genuine befuddlement made me laugh.

"No, they're from the human realm," I explained, moving back into step with him. Dropping my arms back down, I sighed. "It's hard to understand without showing you."

"Then, you will have to show me this fortune cookie." Cheshire slid his hand into mine, smiling at me with a hint of insecurity.

Squeezing his hand, I smiled back. "Of course. Once this is all over, I'd be happy to show you all the delights of the human realm."

Cheshire stroked his thumb across the thin skin between my thumb and forefinger, sending a delicious zing through me. "I will be counting down the moments."

Clearing my throat, I turned my attention back to the path before us. "Oh, look. We're here."

Chess waited for us right before the gate to the Seelie palace. His eyes dipped to our joined hands, but he didn't comment. The guards standing at the gate covered their mouths and shifted away from us as Cheshire came close.

"What is your business here?" One of the golden armored guards asked his hand over his mouth, muffling his words.

The other guard jerked a hand in our direction. "Go away with your disgusting stink."

I huffed and released Cheshire's hand. "We can't. We must see the queen."

"Is she expecting you?" the first guard asked, his eyes watering.

A wicked grin slid up my lips. "Oh, I'm sure she's been informed of our coming. But for the sake of politeness. Tell her, Alice and the Cheshires must speak with her. It is of the utmost importance."

"Important enough not to bathe." The second guard glared at Cheshire.

Cheshire gasped, a hand to his chest. "I bathe quite often. I'll have you know, and I am offended you would suggest otherwise."

Tired of the delay, I added, "He has the sickness and unless you want to get it too, you'll let us in."

Both guards went for their swords, their eyes wide in horror.

"The sickness? In the Underground? Again?" the second guard fumbled over his words, seeming to want to cut us down right there.

The first guard seemed to have more of a head on his shoulders. "You must hurry to the queen. We will spread the word."

"The Moderator is taking those seeking refuge at her home," Chess explained. "Your people can go there as well. She's expecting you."

He nodded and gestured to his fellow guard. They moved away from the entrance allowing us to enter the Seelie palace.

For some reason, my heart was racing. I hadn't been to the Seelie palace since the White Queen locked me away. When they brought me before her, she had just ripped the heart from a Fae. I never found out what his punishment was for, but it didn't set a positive precedent for my sentence. I had, after all, caused her daughter to kill herself.

I remember that moment so clearly—more than any other memory I had.

Her pure white gown and pale skin soaked in the bloody aftermath of the UnSeelie Fae dead at her feet. She had curled her lips in disgust and handed the heart to a nearby servant. Her husband, King Oberon, stood by idly with a bored expression on his face. When the queen saw me, her expression brightened considerably—a wicked grin on her usually cold mouth.

"Oh, Alice. I'm going to enjoy this."

"Hey," Chess bumped me with his shoulder as he walked next to me, his father on my other side. All of us ignoring the Fae in the palaces' reaction to Cheshire's stench as if they were the ones who were out of place.

"Relax." Chess winked at me. "She can't do anything to you now. My kitten might be many things, but she is her mother's daughter. Tatiana won't overstep in fear of losing the little power she has left."

I swallowed and nodded. "Yeah. Right."

I barely noticed the gardens cultivated by Kat on our way into the palace. The inside was just as white and golden as the outside— every wall and floor without a speck of dirt or discoloration. Each piece of furniture placed precisely in the perfect place. It was hard to believe a woman who was so obsessed with perfection would have such a slob for a daughter.

One time, I found Kat with a week's worth of dishes in the sink, eating cereal from the milk jug. She'd just cut the whole top off the jug and filled the half-full jug with cereal instead of actually doing her dishes for once. And don't even get me started on her laundry habits. I didn't know how she had anything to wear most days with how she let them pile up.

Plus, the wrinkles. I shuddered. My mother would have sent me to an early grave if I dared to wear anything with so much as a tiny crease. Kat wore them like a badge of honor. I really didn't get how Chess stood it.

Having distracted myself enough, I was pleased to find we were at the entrance to the Seelie throne room. Another set of guards stood there at attention. Then as if they had been trained to, they proceeded to react the same way the first set of guards had.

"We have an appointment with the queen," Chess announced without giving the guards a chance to question us this time.

They exchanged a questioning look but their desire to get away from the smell overrode their need to do their job. They pulled the doors open and waved us in.

"Well, that went smoothly," I muttered under my breath. "Heaven forbid something goes wrong now."

"Ah, the Great Pretender." An icy voice called out in a sing-song voice. "What brings you to my great court? Come to kill another person I love?"

ALL HAIL THE WHITE QUEEN

I GRIMACED NOT KNOWING how to respond to the Seelie Queen's words. She hadn't said anything untrue but leave it to her to go straight for the gut when attacking one's foe.

Scrounging up my courage, I pressed forward and met Queen Tatiana's icy blue eyes. "Hello, your majesty. How are you?"

Tatiana scowled and flipped her white hair over her shoulder. "Let's not pretend you are here on a social call, Great Pretender." She stepped down the stairs of her dais—her white gown slithering along the floor with every movement.

King Oberon was curiously missing today. Which was all the better for my confidence. The less of an audience I had the better.

Stopping a few feet before me, her a head higher than me, Tatiana surveyed the two felines beside me. "I see you are still playing with the rabble. It's good to know some things haven't changed. Though, your allegiances certainly have."

"I was never on the Shadow Man's side," I argued, tired of having to explain myself all the time.

"Pfft." Tatiana threw her hand up. "No excuses today. You want something from me..." she cooed, her eyes lingering over Chess and Cheshire. "I might give it to you..." her mouth curved up into a seductive smile, "...for a price."

Curling my fingers into tight fists, I stared hard at her, willing her to turn her attention back to me. "No."

"No?" She mused, her eyes turning from the men and back to me. "What do you mean, no? You can't get something for nothing, you know that well, don't you, Alice?"

Pressing my lips into a firm line, I did not waver. "I am not playing by your rules anymore, your majesty. There are more important things at hand now."

"Oh?" Tatiana mused, angling her head to the side. "And what might that be?"

"Information for information," I smiled back at her, parroting her words. "You can't get something for nothing."

Tatiana hummed and placed a hand under her elbow, leaning her face on her other hand. "How do I know that the information you want is worth what you have to give?"

"You'll have to trust me."

Her laughter, like chimes on a windy day, echoed through the throne room. The nearby courtiers and servants chittered with her but cut off abruptly when Tatiana quit laughing. "Why should I ever trust you?"

I leaned forward slightly. "Because you don't have a choice. If you want to save your people and your own neck, that is."

Her brow furrowed and I smirked knowing I had her by the balls as Kat would say.

Knowing she had been bested, Tatiana scoffed and turned her back on me. "I know what you are here for. Your Hatter went into the Bandersnatch. I do not know if he came out again, but you are free to look." She gave me a nasty smile over her shoulder. "I'm sure I can find something to entertain myself. Cheshire...you are looking much better since your time in the Shadow Realm."

Jealousy sparked in my stomach.

"You can't have him," I stepped in front of Cheshire locking eyes with the queen. "And you know your daughter would rip you apart if you even thought about touching her mate."

Tatiana pretended to pout. "Yes, she is quite mean to her own mother. However, you have no such claim on Cheshire and as I'm the one who freed him, I can claim my price whenever I like."

"Hatter already paid the price." Cheshire reminded her behind me.

The queen's brows furrowed. "Yes, well that only counts if he stayed where he was supposed to, but it seemed my cousin's son is far more resourceful than I expected."

"Who?" Cheshire asked.

"The prince," Chess and I told him at the same time.

"So, you can go into the Bandersnatch and I will take my time with the cat, deal?" Tatiana smiled, turning back to us, and taking a few steps forward.

I waited for her to hit Cheshire's aura and with great satisfaction, watched as her eyes widened and her mouth fell open. Her nose scrunched up as she covered her mouth and coughed, quickly backing away.

"What in the world is that smell?"

My lips curled up slowly. "My part of the bargain. Do you recognize that scent? If you were a good queen, you would."

Tatiana glared at me.

The courtiers and servants whispered around us already having guessed where I was going with this.

"The Underground is dying. It's eating away at the magic of its citizens, starting with the weakest," I explained, lifting my voice loud enough for everyone to hear. "If you don't wish to catch the sickness, you should leave the Underground."

"Leave? The Underground?" Different variations of the question went around the room as Tatiana processed my words.

"Cheshire, you have the sickness?"

Smiling broadly, Cheshire bowed mockingly. "A byproduct of the Shadow Realm, I'm sure."

"And yet you are not sickly and weak?" She cocked her head to the side suspiciously.

"We haven't quite figured out that much yet, but we do know others are quite ill. Seer for one," Chess explained for me so Tatiana didn't try to blow this off.

Tatiana went silent as thoughts churned behind her icy gaze. After a moment, she asked, "Have we found a cure? We cannot stay in the human realm forever. They will destroy us."

I inclined my head. "There's a sprout of the Tree of Life but it is not big enough to help right now."

"And of the High King?"

I narrowed my eyes on her. "We have not found someone as of yet to take that place."

Humming to herself, she said, "I see. Well, then," Turning her back to us, she shouted out to the other occupants in the room. "You heard her! The sickness has come once more. Gather your families and head for the Between. We will have to seek sanctuary with the humans until the Underground can regain its magic..." her gaze slid back to me, "...in whatever way necessary."

The people of the court hustled across the throne room, talking loudly as they moved out of the room. Tatiana moved away, dismissing us with a turn of her back.

I stepped forward. "The Bandersnatch."

Tatiana waved me off. "Can't you see I am in the middle of a crisis?" When I didn't budge, she huffed and waved a servant over. "Lead them to my quarters. Make sure they only touch the portal to the Bandersnatch and nothing more. If you don't, I will have your head."

The servant jerked his head in understanding and moved to stand before us. He stopped when he got to the sickness and took a step back. "This way."

Glancing to the others, I wiped my hands on my skirts. My nerves were getting to me. I was so close to getting Mercury back and yet so far.

The trek through the palace and up to the Seelie Queen's bedchamber seemed to drag on and on. I knew, in reality, it had only been a few moments before we stopped before the large double doors to Tatiana's bedroom. My heart jumped into my throat as the servant opened the door for us and ushered us inside.

Tatiana's room was much like the rest of the palace. Neat, almost obsessively so, in colors of gold and white. If I had a choice between spending the rest of my life in the queen's bedroom or the endless Between, the Between would win out every time.

"Her Majesty has graciously allowed you to access the Bandersnatch, do not abuse her mercy." The servant gave us a pointed look and gestured to a wardrobe.

I frowned, approaching the wardrobe. Pulling the doors open, I found myself staring into an inky black mirror. This one was much different than the one in Mab's bedroom. The moment I saw it, my skin prickled, my hairs standing on end, telling me to run away and run now.

Cheshire grabbed my hand, keeping me from touching the surface of the mirror. "Are you sure you want to do this?" His gaze skittered over the mirror, not seeming to like it either. "Hatter may not even be in there anymore. You'd be risking your life for nothing."

I smiled at him and reached out, cupping his cheek with my hand. He leaned into my touch, telling me more about how our relationship had been before now than anything. "Oh, pretty pussycat, if love isn't worth risking your life for, then what is?"

He frowned tightly. "I hate being called that."

Slipping my hand from his, I turned back to the mirror. "I know."

Taking a deep breath, I stepped into the mirror—the inkiness of the mirror surrounding me and making me feel like I was being swallowed whole. When I came out the other side, I knew I had messed up. Mercury wasn't in here. He couldn't be. There was nothing in the space I was in. Not the Bandersnatch. Not Hatter. Not anything.

Spinning around, I tried to go back out the way I came but the mirror was gone. My heart pounded in my chest as I turned one way and then the other, searching the darkness for an exit.

"Hello?" I called out, knowing that I could be attracting something that wanted to eat me. At this point, it was better than nothing.

Silence answered me. I was alone. Utterly, alone in the darkness.

I collapsed to my knees and screamed—the sounds echoing in the distance. Oh, Alice, what have you done now?

About the Author

Come chat me up!
www.erinbedford.com
Facebook.com/erinrbedford
twitter.com/erin_bedford
Don't forget to follow me on Goodreads,
Pinterest, Instagram, and TikTok!

**Want to be the first to know about my
new releases?**
Erinbedford.com/newsletter

Erin Bedford is an otaku, recovering coffee addict, and Legend of Zelda fanatic. Her brain is so full of stories that need to be told that she must get them out or explode into a million screaming chibis. Obsessed with fairy tales and bad boys, she hasn't found a story she can't twist to match her deviant mind full of innuendos, snarky humor, and dream guys.

On the outside, she's a work from home mom and bookbinger. One the inside, she's a thirteen-year-old boy screaming to get out and tell you the pervy joke they found online. As an ex-computer programmer, she dreams of one day combining her love for writing and college credits to make the ultimate video game!

Until then, when she's not writing, Erin is devouring as many books as possible on her quest to have the biggest book gut of all time. She's written over thirty books, ranging from paranormal romance, urban fantasy, and even scifi romance.

www.ingramcontent.com/pod-product-compliance
Lightning Source LLC
Chambersburg PA
CBHW070925190726
48292CB00004B/1109